THE FOUR HORSEMEN: BOUND

L J SWALLOW

Copyright © 2017 by LJ Swallow

Editing by Hot Tree Edits

Cover Designed by Takecover Designs

All rights reserved.

No part of this book may be reproduced in any form or by any electronic or mechanical means, including information storage and retrieval systems, without written permission from the author, except for the use of brief quotations in a book review.

❦ Created with Vellum

To Angel Lawson.
We are levelling up in the marine life game.

1

VEE

*J*oss left.

I'm a light sleeper and often wake as the sun rises, but last night I slept heavily in dreamless darkness. I wake wrapped beneath a blanket, but the man's arms I fell asleep in last night no longer surround me.

I sit up, head in hands, as Ewan's revelation floods my mind again. I waver between disbelief and a strange acceptance towards the news I'm not who I thought I was. The panicked hysteria from hours ago doesn't linger this morning, as if Joss's soothing touch stays with me.

I climb out of bed and peek through the curtains, to ensure some reality still exists. A low mist carpets the ground giving the area surrounding the house an ethereal look, and the sun's barely risen. Still dressed in last night's clothes, I creep out of the room and along the hallway, downstairs towards the back of the house. I reach the kitchen and hold my breath to listen. No noise to indicate anybody else is awake. Right now, I'm happier to be alone with my confused thoughts.

A heavy wooden door at the kitchen rear leads outside to a paved area. A wooden bench overlooks the barren fields, and towards the dense woods, which offer a barrier between the property and the nearest road. I've no desire to run from the house this time, painfully aware running will never be an option.

The sun continues to rise as I sit on the bench and breathe in the morning air. I focus on the familiar: scent of the damp earth and decaying leaves dropped from the beech trees, at the birdsong welcoming me to my new day.

I mull over recent months in my mind. Were there clues? Shortly after Anna left for London, nightmares started. At first, I put them down to the new situation: living alone for the first time. The darkness and screaming in my dreams, along with the breathless fear, which I woke with, gripped me for weeks until the nightmares gradually faded. I still experience the dreams, less frequently, but each time I can never grasp exactly what my subconscious is showing me. The nightmares are always the same, and each time I attempt to recall them I never do, just the darkness.

The other Vee, who believes Ewan lied, interrupts my thoughts. I pull out my phone and scroll through for Anna's number, then send her a friendly "how's things" text. She doesn't reply. My stomach lurches. Does she exist? *Of course she does, it's too early for her to answer the phone yet.*

What did Anna and I do together? I search my mind, but memories of my time with Anna have faded; I can't remember what she looks like. Our teen years, complaining about school and spending all our free time together. The holidays I took with my parents to Spain every year. Did any of that happen?

But, instead of last night's terror, an acceptance floods over. Now the secret's revealed do I need to accept the truth?

To accept I'm not Verity Jameson?

I repeat the words to myself, stunned I'm not freaking out without Joss's calming touch. Honestly, I should be a jabbering mess on the floor.

The door to the house thuds closed, and I look over my shoulder. Heath stands, holding two mugs and a wary expression. He's dressed in the same dark shirt and jeans as last night, and the attraction to him takes over my thoughts as I look back into his green eyes. Reality? He definitely felt real when we kissed; and my reaction was definitely human.

"Hello, Heath."

He crosses and sits on the bench, keeping at a distance to prevent our bodies touching, and hands a mug to me. "I thought you might need a coffee."

"Thanks. You're up early."

"So are you."

"Hmm." I sip the hot liquid, savouring a part of my morning ritual. "Are you surprised?"

"How did you sleep?"

In Joss's arms. "You don't need to avoid the subject,

Heath. I presume you know that last night Ewan told me Verity Jameson doesn't really exist."

He stares at his boots. "Yeah. I know. Ewan and Joss told me how you reacted."

"Are you surprised?" I turn to face him; the concern lining his face tugs away my desire to be cross with him, and I temper my reaction. "I find out I'm part of a mysterious world that I don't understand, mostly because you four hardly tell me anything, and then Ewan decides to tell me the biggest secret of all."

"No. I'm not surprised over how you reacted." Heath folds his warm hand over mine.

I look down. "Let me guess, you were the one sent to talk to me because of our... connection."

Heath's gaze returns to the ground. "Kind of."

How can I say I wish Joss had been the one to approach me, and explain, this morning? That what happened last between Heath and me was between him and the human Verity, the one I need to dismiss and not to be reminded of at this moment? I can't tell Heath, but the truth is I need Joss right now. I want Joss to hold me again and take away the remnants of my confusion. Joss wiped away the weakness the frightening emotions caused, and Heath's bringing those emotions back. Once I'm calmer, I might feel differently, but not now.

I close my eyes. What day is it? Do I need to work today? And Jesus, if somebody chose to put me in this world in disguise, they could've chosen a more interesting job. Or even no job — I would've been perfectly happy tucked away somewhere with wealth and privilege until I was "found."

In a strange reversal, I'm finding it harder to grasp

onto the belief I'm the Verity I thought I was. Insanely, the news I'm not, and I've only existed a short time, sits more comfortably with me.

"How do you feel now?" Heath asks in a soft voice.

I open my eyes, sip more coffee, and shiver in the autumn cool. "I'm forgetting my life already, Heath," I admit. "Suddenly, too, as if somebody pulled the plug and my memories are disappearing down into a whirlpool."

Heath shifts closer and his solid thigh rests against mine. "You must be frightened."

I tense. I don't want him this close to me right now, to add another layer of confusion.

"I was. Now... I don't know. I feel as if a box opened where a part of me was locked away and she's pushing out my memories. Do you think that's what's happened? That this 'real me' was... unleashed." *Oh God.* I hold my head in my hands as my body floods with panic again and focus on the sounds and scents surrounding me. *No. I'm here. I'm me. I'm Verity.*

But I'm not, and the truth rests deep in my soul.

"Maybe," he replies.

I look up, and push hair from my face. "Did the same happen to you and the other guys?"

Heath stares ahead for a few moments, mouth turned down. "No. I don't know where I came from originally. We all arrived at this house on the same day. Literally, woke up one morning, here. Weird shit— we'd never met each other before. I didn't even remember Xander was my brother." He blows air into his cheeks and side glances me. "We had the advantage that we all arrived in the world at once; shared the confusion. I mean, I have a vague memory of agreeing to take on this role, but none of us remember why." He gives a derisive laugh. "In the house, we found a bizarre signed contract where we'd agreed to this. That's it. No specified reward, training, any of that shit. Just a book about our predecessors and some ID. So, yeah, Vee, I partly understand why your head's fucked. "

"You aren't the original Horsemen?" I ask.

"Told you before, that's a warped story."

"I bet your early days are quite a story too."

"A very long one."

His tone shuts down the conversation, and I slump back onto the bench. "I wish somebody had left me some bloody information. Was I in your book?"

"You were alluded to. We thought we were looking for "truth" as a concept, by uncovering deceit in the world. Then Xander announced he was sure you existed in reality and we had to find you."

"What changed his mind? Did somebody tell him?"

Heath shrugs. "Said he had a dream that you were out there and hidden."

"Right. A dream." My doubt matches that I see in his eyes. "But why did whoever hide me?"

"No fucking clue."

We exchange a smile, then sit in silence as I mull over his words. Now I'm self-aware, will they tell me more? "I freaked out and attacked Joss."

"Oh yeah, I heard about that too. I think he has bruises."

"Really?"

"No, I'm kidding. I also heard he slept with you last night." Heath stretches his long legs out and taps his boot toes together. "I always hoped it would be my bed you spent the night in."

"I've slept in Joss's bed before."

"Not with him though."

"Believe me, there was nothing romantic about it—or anything else."

"Yeah, but he was there to help. Joss was the one who made things better for you." Heath turns his eyes to mine. "I wish I'd been there for you."

"But that's his power, right? He was helping me."

"I doubt that's all it is." Heath drains his mug and stands, mouth set firm. "Anyway, I'm hungry. Want me to cook you breakfast?"

His response irritates me; he should be happy Joss was there to help. "Sure. Then I can get ready for work."

"Work?" Heath's expression is as if I told him demons had breached the house's defences.

"I thought we agreed I could work?" I ask.

"I don't think Xander agrees."

"Screw Xander."

Heath chokes a laugh. "I think you two are going to have an 'interesting' relationship."

"Hey, whatever I am, Vee still exists. and she doesn't take bad attitude from people. Especially not guys." I pause. "I need to be the Vee who works at Alphanet, just for a few hours. Can you explain that to him, please?"

"Okay. And for the record, I think you'll need that attitude around my brother." I follow as he yanks open the door to the house.

Inside the kitchen, the smell of cooked bacon hits me and my stomach rumbles. Joss stands at the stove, spatula in hand.

"Just in time! I cooked breakfast. Nothing like bacon to make the world a happier place." A smile crinkles the corners of his eyes. "How are you this morning, Vee?"

"Better," I say cautiously.

"Cool." He blows his blond fringe from his eyes. "Want some too, Heath?"

I glance at an unimpressed Heath and nudge him. "Famine making breakfast. Funny, huh?"

"Yeah, he's quite the cook. I don't eat breakfast." Heath inclines his head to the hallway. "If you want to head to work today, I'll get dressed and take you."

I chew my lip as I watch him leave. Heath told me he was hungry. Did Joss ruin his appetite?

Joss dumps the bacon on a chipped plate and slides it along the kitchen counter towards me. "Has Heath explained things?"

"Not much. I don't feel like talking about it again."

He nods and drops bacon on a plate for himself. "I want you to know I'm here if you need help coping. A hug or whatever." He cocks a brow. "Distraction."

Joss's words are the opposite of Heath's heavy conversation. "You know what?" I say. "I think your Joss-ness helps. I don't mean the guy who calms me when I'm around him, but the joking."

He pouts. "I'm not joking. I'd take you upstairs and 'distract' you if you clicked your fingers."

I focus on creating a sandwich from the nearby bread and search for an answer to give him. None comes. As I meet his eyes, I lick bacon grease from my fingers, and he watches the action before taking my hand from my mouth.

"Don't do that," he mutters.

"What?"

But Joss doesn't need to reply, and in my calmer state, his touch is the opposite to soothing. He touches my face. "After you fell asleep last night, I left you because holding you drove me nuts. Do you realise you smell better than bacon, and that's pretty damn impossible?" I smile and he shakes his head, as if shaking away a thought. "Anyway, the four of us talked about the 'situation'. We decided Heath should be the one who spoke to you. And about Ewan... be nice to him. He feels like shit about what he did."

"Ewan? I don't blame him. I mean, yeah the news could've been broken more diplomatically, but he didn't mean to hurt me. I'm sure of that."

Joss bites his lip. "The other thing we decided is to give you a hundred percent control over what you want to happen."

I snort. "I bet Xander loved that idea."

"Actually, it was his suggestion. Xander's worried that you'll run now. You're crucial to us as the missing piece. We need you to stick around. If you want anything from any of us, ask." He bows, flourishing his hands in front of him. "We're here to carry out your every whim."

I take a bite from my sandwich. This is what I mean. The joking Joss is who I need, the way I've discovered that I need Ewan's forthrightness and Heath's gentleness. In a way, I also need Xander's control of the situation, although that doesn't sit as well with me.

I swallow the mouthful. "Thanks for the sandwich."

"Any time," he says softly. "Just say the word."

As Joss straightens, a realisation hits. When the human memories ebbed, something else flowed in to replace them. The bond to these four men is stronger than I imagined, and an idea I dismissed until now crystallises.

My heart and soul are open to all four of the guys, and with that, the confusion from the last few days sharpens into reality.

I not only *want* them all, but I *have* them all.

2

VEE

I hate to admit this, because I don't want him to be, but Xander's right. Work is a world away from my new life, and sitting in a cubicle answering queries feels insignificant after the last forty-eight hours.

Heath and I rushed to arrive on time after the decision was made to work, which means I didn't see Ewan and Xander before we left. I worry about Ewan after Joss's words. Ewan last saw me in a hysterical mess he was partly responsible for, and the regret on his face sticks with me. Xander... hmm. Not so sorry I missed him.

Heath works in a different part of the building to me, so we part ways at the elevators. With our passionate encounter yesterday evening now pushed down by the events that followed, I engage in mundane conversation before we separate, although the false brightness must be apparent to everybody else crammed in the elevator with us.

Heath texts a couple of times to check up on me. Joss does too, which isn't a surprise. I smile to myself when the second message from Joss arrives while I'm by the water cooler, and I glance over at Charlotte and Victoria. They can lust over Heath, but not only do I have him, but also his equally hot friend. My fingers itch to type back a request for Joss to meet me after work and flaunt in the girls' faces that both guys are in my life and care for me.

One day I should allow myself to be seen with both of them, in the Clone Club's vicinity, of course. Or maybe all four of my new harem. My smile grows, amused by the thought and the word, and I return to my desk.

For today, I'll have to make do with Heath as a lunch date. *Make do*. Ha ha.

At lunch, I head to the cafeteria where Heath stands outside, facing away from me, hands in suit pockets. He draws looks from girls passing, as ever, but remains oblivious. Yep, ass still awesome in a suit. I have mixed emotions as I look at him. First, the instant arousal from remembering how his hands felt on my skin and how intoxicating he tasted, but trepidation joins because I'm walking away from my fading human life and into my new one with each moment I spend with him.

I poke Heath as I approach, and he blinks around at me. "Hey," I say.

"Vee." He kisses my cheek, and I freeze in surprise.

Friendly. Caring. Not a sign he wants to pin me to the wall and continue our activities from last night.

"You okay?" he asks. "You look flushed."

I touch my cheek with the back of a hand. "Warm in here."

"Uh huh." His knowing smile confirms what I suspected—Heath is aware of the effect he has on girls.

We head into the cafeteria, and I fight giving a little wave to Charlotte who turns from the cashier holding a tray with her solitary salad wrap and bottle of water. She blinks, barely disguising her disbelief, before walking over to a table to sit with her friends. No Victoria? Perhaps she's working on her hair.

Shiny wooden round tables and chairs dot around the place, some occupied by fellow employees on phones, or others chatting, and my stomach rumbles at the smell of fried food. Bacon for breakfast? I suppose I should pick a healthier lunch.

We choose a quiet corner, and I sit on the hard chair, avoiding the fake Yucca plant attacking my head. Heath heads off to order and returns with a plate piled with burger and chips for him, and a salad for me. I watch with curiosity as he digs in. Do Horsemen genes stop massive weight gain? Is chasing demons a good workout?

"What do we have planned for this evening?" I ask as I pick up my cutlery. "Demons need killing? Trip to the pub? Maybe you could introduce me to some werewolves?"

"Vee," he growls in warning. "Keep your voice down."

"You guys really need to lighten up."

Heath gives a despairing shake of his head. "Sure, Vee."

"Can we talk?" I ask

"What did you want to talk about?" Heath's discomfort

level ramps up as worry crosses his face. "I can't really explain anymore about your... origins."

"Not last night, don't worry. Or the other issue between us. We already had that awkward conversation."

We sure did. As with last time, Heath's "act as if nothing happened" show started, and on the way here, I called him out on the behaviour. The short exchange didn't touch on how intense the situation was for the pair of us, and it ended with an agreement not to touch each other again.

Not to touch in the same way, at least.

Or soon, anyway.

Well, maybe in the future.

Ah, crap.

"You guys talk about something called the Order. What's the Order? Is this all connected to the demons holding power?"

"The Order?" Heath lowers his voice and I look around the cafeteria. Everybody's too engrossed in their own world to worry about ours. "The Order is the name for the demon-led organisation in the world. Their activity criss-crosses and tangles every area of human society in a web." He draws on the table with his fingers as he talks. "It's an umbrella term because the Order's split into many cells present in most countries. They influence governments or control business and financial institutions, but they're also found in lower level roles. Law enforcement, medical, even schools. You name any part of society, and there'll be a demon influence in there somewhere."

"How the hell are four of you supposed to deal with that?"

Heath bites down on a chip. "We can't deal with everything. That's why we're allied with the other races who exist here. Nobody wants a world taken over by demons; the humans won't be the only ones wiped out or enslaved. After what happened with Portia, seems our alliances have become shaky."

I stare back, unable to find words as I attempt to process all this.

"Our main role is to keep the portals closed and prevent more demons arriving. A side role involves interrupting communication and planning between the demons who exist here already, or stepping in for damage control."

"Damage control?"

"Preventing attacks on humans, small scale or large scale."

Wow. "How widespread is the demon influence?"

"Wide. Getting wider. We can't keep on top of this without the help of those on our side. That's why this fuck-up with the fae doesn't help."

I recognise the self-blame on Heath's face and place a hand over his. "Heath. Your killing the fae attacking me was orchestrated and so was the attack on Portia."

"Doesn't change the ripples it causes." He sinks back and runs his hands through his hair, elbows at right angles

His words exhaust me; the juggling the guys do hurts my head. "Let me get this straight. You're here to keep portals closed. And keep the peace between supernatural races. *And* investigate and stop demon corruption."

He raises both brows. "Fun, huh?"

"Whoa. No wonder you need a Fifth. Surprised you don't need another fifteen."

"The portals are safe currently; we haven't seen major activity around any in months. Plus, the keeping the peace part isn't too hard. Usually. Like I said, we have help, but we never totally trust people. The biggest problem? We may need to ally with those we don't want to, if this gets any worse."

Does he mean demons? I don't voice the question, but Portia mentioned that too. But there's one question, bigger than all my others. "Heath, what happens if the Horsemen fail?"

Heath clenches his jaw and looks behind me. "I have no fucking clue."

I bite inside my cheek. Why did I ask that? He's already told me they only vaguely understand their own situation. Heath pulls out his phone, brow tugged, and switches his attention from me. Ordinarily, this rude behaviour would irritate me, but I've pushed him too far out of what he can cope with.

3

Vee

I'm relieved when I return from work and back into my new life. All day I studied faces around me, worried another demon, or fae, or goodness-knows-what lurked, waiting for an opportunity to attack me. I know I have a power, but no clue how to use it yet. My self-defence skills failed against a demon once, and even with Death close by to back me up, I doubt my chances.

I don't want to be alone with my thoughts and head downstairs as soon as I change from my work uniform. Black leggings and a baggy blue jumper suit the cool farmhouse, and I pull on thick socks too. What am I supposed to spend evenings doing? I guess laptop and TV is my usual entertainment, but that was the old Verity.

Old Verity. The desire to examine my face in the mirror, to cement in my mind who I am, drops as the hours pass and the old Vee fades. How? How can somebody or something create false memories and put me here? And why the hell are those memories fading this quickly?

Worse than that, how am I readily accepting the situation?

I walk into the kitchen where the guys examine a large map spread across the pine table, files of paper and an open book either side of Xander, who's central to the group. Heath stands behind him, arms crossed over his broad chest; Ewan beside Xander, laptop open glancing between the map and screen. Joss sits on the table with his feet on a chair, the other side of Xander, reading the map upside down.

Hell, these men are hot. Individually, I can almost cope, but seeing them together like this addles my brain. I don't think that's only the "power of the Five," or whatever this is, but a normal, female physical reaction to them. They don't notice me at first as I flick my gaze from guy to guy.

Heath's long legs in his perfect-fitting jeans are as distracting as the sensuous mouth that kissed me. I switch to looking at Ewan's deep-browed concentration and the broad-chested, tattooed body I'd love to explore. Then there's Joss's lithe figure hinting at toned muscle beneath and the way his eyes shine when he looks at me. And Xander... Why does he have to rank as high on the heat metre? Forget his killer body and the pursed lips I half fantasise about kissing to shut him up, but his presence exudes a sexuality as raw as the anger I've seen in him.

Were they created too? Heath said he chose to take this role, which means in the past, he was somebody else. Are they from a magical gene pool that creates heart-stoppingly gorgeous men?

I inhale and convince myself the dizziness is from that and not my intoxication by the guys.

"Old school?" I ask.

"What do you mean?" Xander looks up at me, finger resting on a map location. The exhausted look from yesterday has lifted, his eyes brighter and the stress doesn't emanate from him the way it did. I compare him to his brother. Same eyes, same symmetrical faces, but Xander's lighter brown hair and shorter style set them apart.

I point. "Paper maps."

"This is an old map we're comparing to Google maps," retorts Xander.

Okay, I was wrong; he's as "friendly" as ever.

"Evening, Vee." Joss waves at me. He's dressed in green cargo pants, a black T-shirt beneath a plaid shirt and feet bare. His smile brings down my anxiety a notch as usual, and I move to stand next to him. "Nice day at work?"

I pull a face. "I think I should give up work. I don't think they appreciate my new role saving the world," I say tongue in cheek.

"Told you," replies Xander as he squints at the map.

Ewan's focus remains on his laptop, and my forgiveness for his big mouth switches to irritation that he's refusing to acknowledge me.

I spot the half-empty bottles lined up on the table. "Is

that how you fuel your powers? Do I need to become a beer drinker too?"

Joss grins and I swear Xander fights a smile too. "Yup. You'd better get started."

"I'm not a hundred percent sure you're joking." I take a bottle from the table and swig before pulling a face. "Nope. I prefer cider."

"Ugh!" protests Heath. "Really?"

Ewan's continued silence, and refusal to look at me, continues to niggle.

"So, what are you looking for?" I ask them and hand the beer to Joss.

"Ley lines are marked on old maps. Demons often base themselves where the lines intersect because they can draw on the power. We're checking what's built over the lines nowadays by comparing with Google street view," explains Heath.

"Ley lines?" I ask.

"Lines between places in the world that carry positive or negative energy from the earth. A matrix of them across the world was mapped out in the past. So where two or more lines converge, you have a place of great power and energy. That's what we're looking for," replies Heath

"Okay." Red and blue lines cross a creased map of the UK, spots where they cross annotated in black ink. Wanting a clearer view, I stand behind Xander and Ewan, besides Heath.

Close to the four, something unexpected happens. Images crash into my mind, different to the strange darkness and blood ones. This place is brighter, blinding the faces and surroundings out of focus. Pain stabs behind my eyes, joined by the same fear as the shadowy nightmares.

I jerk as Heath touches my arm. "Are you okay, Vee?"

"I think memories are trickling back. Real ones, I mean."

I glance at Ewan and a muscle in his cheek twitches, but he doesn't look up.

Subject change needed. "Is this where the portals are that you need to protect?" I ask and point at the map.

"No. There're seven in different parts of the world and tightly sealed. There's one in the UK but not around here," says Xander. "The portals aren't our worry right now, but they could be if there's a combined attack on them. The demons' ultimate aim is to open them, which is why we deal with the bastards at ground level before they amass enough power."

"Such as adding in some fae power by recruitment," puts in Joss. "That's partly what this situation is about. Persuade enough fae to switch alliances and they've more power at their disposal."

"Okay." Their words panic and confuse me; there's so much I only half-understand.

Xander turns in his seat and studies me. "By the way, sorry about last night. When I'm worked up, and in combat mode, I find it hard to calm down afterwards. My mouth runs away sometimes too, ask the guys."

"Often," says Joss with a laugh. "We ignore him. You should too."

"Don't let my brother give you any crap though," says Heath.

"I doubt she's about to take any, especially after last night," says Joss.

"How's that going?" asks Xander.

"The 'I'm not real' thing?"

"That and discovering you have powers." I'm unsure whether to be annoyed or pleased by his nonchalance compared to the other guys' concern.

"I'm okay. I don't know why, but I feel as if I'm me now. I'm losing track of the old Verity." Ewan's eyes finally meet mine; troubled, wary

"Interesting," says Xander. "If you're cool with the situation, that's good."

Ewan rubs fingertips along his lips but doesn't speak. "I'm cool with it," I say in his direction.

In a room surrounded by the Horsemen, the realisation who I am and the awareness I belong with them grows. I doubted their crazy stories at first, but from day one, I was pulled into the circle rather than left on the edge.

"Right, back to this," says Xander. He reads out coordinates and then cranes his neck to read Ewan's screen. "Any activity up there?"

Whoa. Conversation about Verity over, then?

"Just fields," Ewan replies.

"Hmm. Farm? Property?"

"Managed Access." He looks at me. "Usually means there is or was Ministry of Defence activity there. Firing ranges and such."

"We should check the area out anyway," replies Joss. "Sometimes government facilities aren't on the maps; the demons could be based in an old military building."

"Nah, too far to drive today." Xander follows a line with his finger. "These lines converge on the edge of a small village. Has that area grown to include more houses?"

Ewan taps laptop keys. "Yeah. It's Grangeton outskirts."

Xander straightens. "Interesting. What's there?"

"I can't tell. The street view shows a row of buildings, some office and some shops I guess. Could be any."

Xander pulls on his bottom lip. "Right, we need to check the place out, but we also need to follow up the information we have from Elyssia. Both need doing before too much time passes and the bastards move on."

Elyssia. "Is Portia okay?" I ask.

"She'll be fine. They've upped the security around Portia, but I'm worried that won't be enough if enemies are close to her." Xander tips his chair back and drinks his beer. "I went to see her with Joss today, not that we were welcome. Talk about bloody ungrateful."

"We managed to get a lead from Elyssia while we were there," puts in Joss.

Xander drops the chair back onto four legs. "A vague one. Elyssia claims she doesn't know much about Hunter. She met him at a club with her friends and they struck up an uh... 'friendship.'"

"What about Hunter's friends?" asks Heath. "Did she meet any of his?"

Xander shakes his head. "Elyssia sent me a photo of Hunter from her phone and told us which club she met him in. I want to head down to the place and speak to Arlo."

I pull out a chair and sit. "Stop right there."

Xander frowns at me. "What?"

"Don't start discussing everything as if I know who

and what you're talking about. Which club? Who's Arlo?" I ask.

"A club called The Warehouse. He's a fae and owns the place, but human lackeys run the joint." Xander's response is curt and dismissive. "Often the place attracts supes, especially younger ones, and we visit once in a while to check things out, especially if there've been local attacks."

"And this is a bloody big attack," puts in Joss.

"And you think this guy, Arlo, might know the demons involved?"

Heath laughs. "Doubt it. He doesn't like trouble."

"Such as the Horsemen interfering with his clientele," Joss adds. "He keeps an eye on what's happening in the area for us, so he's either missed the signs or knows more. We need to find out which."

"So what? Are we headed down there tonight?" asks Heath.

"Not all of us. I want two of us to check out these places the ley lines cross, and two of us can head to the club. I think Joss and you should go check out these buildings." He taps a place on the map where lines cross. "Joss can detect demons quicker, and you can kill a few in one go if needed, Heath. I'll take Ewan to The Warehouse."

"What about me? I'm not staying here on my own!" I protest.

"Who'd you prefer to go with?" Xander asks.

Talk about trapped between a rock and a hard place. I hate clubs, but also I don't like the idea of being dragged into the cold looking for demonic creatures.

"Go to the club," says Joss. "Less dangerous because

it's more public. Besides, you can watch Xander's diplomacy in action." He ends his sentence with a laugh and pats Xander on the head.

Xander rubs his head and scowls at Joss. "At least one of us can stay focused with everything happening."

"And I suppose by 'everything happening' you mean me?" I retort.

Xander ignores my question. "Come with me and Ewan tonight." He picks up his phone and checks the time. "Best get yourself ready."

I huff and stare at the ceiling again. There's no way I'll understand all this without walking into and experiencing these situations. I could sit here for the rest of the day and their talk of the Order, portals, demons, and the crazy world around me wouldn't make sense.

I think I'm in for one huge learning curve.

4

EWAN

Tonight I'm supposed to be on full alert for demon and fae activity at the club, but the only thing that has me on alert right now is Vee.

The whole time she's spent with us, Vee's worn slouchy clothes. Her long legs and cute ass look amazing in jeans, that's undeniable, but Vee in a dress ready to visit a club?

Mind wrecking.

Does she understand the effect she has on the four of us? I've no idea if Heath and Vee kissed again—or more. Nothing about their behaviour in public indicates they have, but I have my doubts. But Vee could never be mine—or any of ours—because we all belong to each other. Where will that lead?

Vee slept with Joss last night when I fucked up, but he

told us nothing happened. I believe him based on the mess she was in, and Joss being the guy he is wouldn't take advantage.

But he held her, and she wanted him to.

Fuck, Ewan. Jealousy won't work in this situation.

I hold my breath as Vee approaches me. Tight black dress reaching above her knees, heels impractical for the environment she's walking into, and a small jacket pulled in at the waist. Her hair's loose, touching the exposed skin above the low-cut dress. She disguised her usual natural look with smoky eyes and shining lips; I bite mine as I imagine doing the same to hers.

"Looking good, Vee," calls Joss. "Wish I was the one going out for a night with the hot chick!"

"You have your job for the night, Joss, and that job isn't hitting on Vee again," retorts Xander.

Joss pulls a mock-offended face and clutches his chest. "I am perfectly respectable around our beautiful Fifth."

"Then don't call me a hot chick," replies Vee with a scowl.

Heath wanders from the house. "I don't see why we can't all go to The Warehouse. We could check out the other places tomorrow."

"I told you, this is time sensitive. Plus, we split up in case someone wants all of us in one place again," replies Xander. "Ewan's the only one of you three who doesn't constantly look at Vee as if he wants to tear her clothes off. I'm not interested either, so it makes sense we go to the club with her."

Can Vee tell he's lying? Because I bloody can.

"Ha. You're just looking for a hook up, Xan," laughs

out Joss. "Once you're satisfied there aren't any demons at the club, you'll look for a different kind of satisfaction, right?"

"Whatever, dude."

Vee takes our constant banter better than I expected she would. This time, she turns her eyes skyward in amusement before she looks over and gives me her heart-wrenching smile.

A night with Vee is going to kill me.

"We travel separately," Xander says as he hits the button to unlock his car. "Safer in case one of us has to leave while the other stays."

Xander's lovingly cared for red Aston Martin is parked beside Heath's SUV, my bike, and Joss's Audi hatchback. The Aston stands out wherever we go, and Xander takes his car whenever he can. Flashy bastard. He had a choice of cars he could've bought to shout prestige, but his decision to drive an Aston Martin adds to his cultivated image: English guy who's rough around the edges despite his cultured accent.

I wheeled my motorbike out from the garage earlier. Screw his Aston; I wouldn't swap my Moto Guzzi for anything. No Harley for me; I'm not part of anybody's crowd but my own. I don't want wannabe bikers passing on Harleys and acknowledging me as if I'm part of them.

When I need breathing space away from these three, this bike can move fucking fast and wherever the hell I like.

Vee's short dress stops me asking if she'd like to ride with me.

"Nice bike," she says. "I don't know much about them

but, uh, big and shiny and great for outrunning demons, I guess?"

"I think he tries to downplay his geek image," says Joss with a laugh.

"Geek image?" She runs a look the length of me. "Tattooed guy in a leather jacket? Not my classification of a geek."

Vee's defence of my status amuses me. "I'll give you a ride when you're more suitably dressed," I tell her.

"I'd like that."

And she smiles that smile again, the one to fill and break my heart.

XANDER

Alone time with Little Miss Truth at last.

She climbs into the car beside me and straightens her dress, pulling the material to reach her knees.

I watch with interest. Hell, this girl will attract a lot of attention tonight. I half wish she'd chosen to go with the other two guys. I'm not in the mood to watch Vee closely; she'd better not freak out once we're at the club. Vee's already uncomfortable, and we haven't arrived yet. But she's too big a distraction for Joss and Heath, and not just because they'd probably compete for her attention, but because they're too protective of Verity.

Verity who isn't Verity. *That* nugget of information

was one to stay quiet about for a few days. If I hadn't been tightly wound after taking out the demons at Portia's house, I wouldn't have lost my temper when she challenged me a few hours later. If I hadn't hinted at her true history, Ewan would never have opened his mouth and dropped the truth on her from a fucking big height.

I lost my shit when Ewan told me and Heath what he'd said; and I stayed up half the night ready and waiting to stop her leaving if she tried. I'm stunned she didn't; again the guys don't give her enough credit. Vee's strong. But is she hiding her real feelings about how this affects her, or did we do Vee and her situation a favour?

Mine and Vee's original introduction could've gone better, but I didn't have time for niceties. I have a job, she has a job, we took down the attackers. Maybe I shocked the hell out of Vee, but we succeeded. End of.

I swear she covers the other three in "stupid" every time she's around them. They knew she had a power, that Vee isn't some human chick who needs protecting, but they treat her like she's as delicate as she looks. When I held Vee's hand and her power amplified mine, the physical intensity also flowing between us couldn't be denied, but this is how it will be. The Four are supposed to centre ourselves around Verity, but because she's Truth, not because she's a girl whose legs and ass knock me dead in the dress she chose tonight.

Yeah, I see their problem, the sexual energy's around me and Vee now, but I don't want to let this interfere. Seriously, I'm not getting involved in any "see who can screw Vee first" competition. One focus: I—we—have a job to do, and so does she.

I start the engine, the car purring to life, as I

straighten my arms on the wheel and feel the power biting on the clutch beneath my foot. I speed away from the house and onto the dark lane; Vee grips the edge of the seat as I swerve across the road.

"Don't worry, I'm a good driver," I say.

"I'm fine, just happy you don't ride actual horses, otherwise I'd fall off if you rode like this." She tips a wry smile in my direction.

Not wanting conversation in case she asks me a million and one questions, I shake my head and keep driving.

The journey into Grangeton takes half an hour; the first half spent in relative silence as I'm lost in planning: how to deal with any demon we find, and if we do which sort are they likely to be? Have we brought the right weapons? How will Vee react if we're confronted again? I can't have the girl freezing in fear.

"I don't go to clubs often," she says.

"I bet you don't go to ones like this," I reply. "An interesting clientele. I'd call them Goths, but I've no clue what they'd call themselves. Their music's shit, that's for sure." Vee laughs. "The vamps pick up donors from places like this."

"Donors?" Her amusement stops abruptly. "Ewan mentioned that the vampires were under control."

"Yeah, mostly. The vamps have their human donor partners who they're supposed to stick with. Some younger ones don't always comply because they like to experiment, and that's when some trouble for us to deal with appears. Arlo allows vamps into his club when he thinks we're not looking. I think that's too dangerous."

Vee shifts in her seat, the dress riding up her legs

distracting me. If I stay focused on my current job, I don't succumb to her. Hell, that sounds crap. She has no intention of forcing us to *succumb,* but the daily struggle is real. Joss is right. I need to get laid because walking around wanting Vee isn't helped by the need to get sex out of my system.

"Right."

Hopefully that shut her up for now.

I grip the steering wheel and look ahead again. No. She needs info. "There's a chance you could meet any of the following as they're the other kind often drawn to the place. Imps, incubi, or succubi. Plus fae of course."

"Imps? Like little fairies?"

"Whoa! Don't say that in front of the fae. Hell, they're demons. More annoying than dangerous, but not welcome. Don't you know anything about this stuff?'

Vee narrows her eyes at me. "I know what incubi and succubi are. I bet they fight with the vampires."

"Huh?"

"They both feed off humans, yes?"

"Yeah. They both kill too, so keep away."

"But not me." I raise a brow at her confidence. "Right?"

"Did the guys say nobody could kill you or something?" I ask. The roads become brighter lit as we leave countryside behind for the town's outskirts. Vee doesn't reply, and I smack my forehead. "Seriously, aren't you pissed off those three didn't tell you everything?"

"They said we're all immortal. Which means nobody can kill us."

"Permanently."

"Yes, which makes me immortal."

"Immortal. Definition: never dying or decaying. Not: can't be killed."

"That's very confusing and contradictory."

"And painful at times." I bite back the joke when her face pales. "Part of Heath's job."

Vee's mouth parts and she blinks. "Can he resurrect people?"

Oh for fuck's sake. "I have an idea, Vee. Should I write you a 'Guide to the Four Horsemen and Your Place in Their Lives'?"

"Very funny. I've read about the Horsemen online and none of it matches you."

"Haven't you seen enough of what we do to see we're both ends of the spectrum? Joss starves people but in a positive way too." I pause. "As you know from the night you spent with him."

Verity looks down at her hands, pink tingeing her cheeks. Aha. She does have a thing for Joss; now I need to figure out if she acted on the "thing."

"Me? I'm a peacemaker as well as troublemaker." I side glance her. "Though you haven't seen the peacemaking yet."

"Definitely not. You're very aggressive."

"And do you like me when I'm not?" I throw her my look, the slow smile that catches girls' attention.

She pokes her tongue in her cheek. "A little."

I slap my hands on the wheel and chuckle. "I love that you have to be diplomatic because you can't lie. Which little bit of me do you like?"

Vee narrows her eyes at me. "The part I have to."

"Too funny! No straight answer from you." I shake my head. "I'm sure you'll like me eventually. Most girls do."

"But I'm not a girl, remember?"

"Ha! Smart answer." I smile to myself as I pull the car into the darkened car park behind the shipping containers, and outside the club. I never expected to like Vee. Yes, I knew how important she was, and when Truth came up in our research, I cheered that we had a way to meet the growing problem in the world, but I was really pissed off when I discovered Truth was a chick. A female amongst the four of us? Not good. And no, I'm not a chauvinist, but a realist.

As typical guys, we've not had a conversation over how Vee affects us; I don't think we need to. What she does is clear—she amplifies *everything* and not just our powers. She's the Fifth and at the centre.

What would happen if we united?

I run my tongue along my lip as she climbs out the car, unable to draw my eyes away from her shapely ass. Uniting with Vee? I might be able to resist the effect she has on me, but only if I concentrate really bloody hard.

Although, concentrating on her backside and allowing naked Vee images into my mind isn't helpful.

I step out of the car and shrug on my jacket. Her eyes meet mine, uncertainty in them. Both our barriers are softened from being in the small space with her, and I'm unsure that's a good thing.

The other guys might want to chase around after her. Me? I'll wait for Vee to come to me.

5

Vee

I stand by the Aston Martin, which Xander parked in the shadows, hidden between two shipping containers in the corner of the lot and away from the nearby warehouses.

"Don't you think your car's a bit conspicuous?" I ask him as he looks at me over the roof of the car.

"And? Why does that matter?"

"People—demons—will know you're around if they see your car. Aston Martins are expensive and unusual."

"And cool as fuck, right? Maybe I want them to know I'm around. Besides, once I'm this close anybody I'm pursuing won't have a chance to run far, especially with more than one of us around."

"But, still..."

Xander slams the door closed. "You ask questions

about the weirdest things. This car looks awesome and moves fucking fast. End of."

"Wow, okay, Mr. Attitude." I turn away from him. What have I done to him that causes him to be this rude? I dismiss taking his attitude personally. From what I've witnessed, this behaviour isn't only directed at me.

"Am I dressed okay?" I ask, sudden self-awareness hitting to match the cold slapping my legs.

Xander's slow appraisal sets the familiar tingle along my spine as his green eyes meet mine. "I don't think you'll stand out too much with what you're wearing. Have you much experience in dealing with overfriendly guys, though? This is a club. Political correctness won't apply and hands might wander."

"I can look after myself," I say, and he nods, but his expression doesn't support his agreement.

We cross the uneven ground between the darkened parking area and approach the warehouse building housing the club. Music thuds from inside and through a doorway, the door painted black and squeezed between two other buildings. A painted sign above reads, imaginatively, "The Warehouse." People hang around outside, talking in groups or bunched together as they pass into the venue. Relief wipes away some apprehension as some girls' dress resembles mine: dark clothes, short and tight. Others wear skintight jeans, many with interesting hair colour choices.

Even better, nobody pays any attention to us.

A man rests against the wall outside, smoking, as he stares at his feet. I tense and halt, as he shifts and the dim light above the door catches his blue hair.

Xander looks down at me. "Yes, he's fae and from

Portia's locality. Same as your attacker the other night, but don't stress, I know him."

Uh huh. Right. No stress here.

Xander approaches the guy, and I hang back as they hold a low conversation. Wrapping my arms around myself, I watch two girls in short skirts and high boots enter the building.

I look back in the car park's direction. Where's Ewan? I didn't notice him behind us when we drove here, but surely he can't be far behind?

Xander beckons me over and gestures. "Verity, this is Ronan."

Ronan mirrors Xander's earlier slow appraisal of me and runs his fingers along his bottom lip. Obviously he isn't the same person as my attacker, but his tall, wiry frame and violet eyes trigger an anxious memory.

"Hey, Verity. Great to finally meet you. I heard a lot about you."

"Who from?" I ask hastily.

"Portia. She mentioned the Fifth was with the Horsemen the day she was attacked, and helped save the day, so now we're extra curious about you."

I stare back, unsure how to respond.

"You're freaked out by how I look, aren't you? I've nothing to do with the guy your friend Heath killed. We haven't figured out who that was yet."

"Surely you've noticed someone's missing?" asks Xander.

Ronan rests against the wall and pushes his feet forward. "A few of our guys are missing; he could be one of half a dozen. Our council told everybody they've been abducted, and fae would never side with demons, but the dead guy's actions contradict that."

"Why did they want to... take me or whatever?" I ask.

"Same reason these behind the plot attacked Portia," replies Ronan. "They want to interfere with the Horsemen's control over the portals and therefore the world. You're key to their fight. Nobody knows for sure how or why yet, but you're pretty damn important. That's why they've tried to get hold of you before the Horsemen found you."

I shiver at the implication behind "get hold of," and Xander's silence worries me. Ronan pulls himself from the wall and claps Xander on the back. "But, we have other things on our mind tonight, right, Xan?"

Xander shrugs his arm away. "I'm here in a professional capacity."

Ronan tips his head. "There's a smoking-hot new barmaid."

"There's a smoking-hot new barmaid every time I visit," replies Xander with a sly grin.

"All looking for a piece of Xander." Ronan slings an arm around Xander's shoulders. "Man, I had my eye on this one for a couple of weeks and here you are, ready to cockblock me."

Xander chuckles. "Not my intention, man. But what can I say? I'm irresistible."

Seriously? I shuffle from foot to foot uncomfortable by their conversation. Perhaps Joss is right and Xander's motives tonight *are* only half professional.

"Go on in." Ronan gestures to the door.

"What about Ewan?" I ask.

I've listened for his bike's arrival the whole time I

waited, but no other vehicle has appeared in the darkened car park. Ewan left before us; surely he should be here?

"Knowing Ewan, he probably took the scenic route," says Xander. "Let's go. He'll find us."

Xander slides an arm around my waist, and I look up at him in surprise. He hasn't touched me since the afternoon at Portia's house. A surprise intensity burns in his eyes as his touch spreads warmth into me. He clearly responds the same way to me as I do to him, despite our mutual ambivalence.

"I think it's better people think we're together," he explains. "If that's okay with you."

I'm hyperaware of where his hip rest against mine, and the arousal growing due to his long fingers against my waist. This is ridiculous; I hardly like the man.

Xander leans in to whisper, "I promise not to grope your ass."

"You'll regret it if you do," I hiss and remove his arm from my waist.

Xander sighs. "Hold my hand instead then."

I hesitate before I place mine in his, hoping I don't experience the blinding, shattering reaction from last time. Nothing. But Xander's tight grip is accompanied by a desire to keep my hand in his, despite several seconds ago not wanting him anywhere near me. This is bloody weird, again.

A huge venue filled with smoke and disorientating strobe lights greets us as we walk through the doorway. There're two floors, and the entrance is at the top. Below, a large bar runs the length of the right-hand wall, surrounded by stools and people. A throng below writhe together to the heavy industrial music; bodies packed tightly.

"We need to go that way," calls Xander in my ear, indicating left. "A guy called Declan manages the place. Arlo likes to keep a distance between his ownership and involvement in the day to day. Declan's my first point of contact, and he should be in his office."

"Okay," I shout back.

"Unless you want a drink first?" He gestures downstairs as I struggle to hear his words.

I shake my head and call, "Let's get this over with."

Xander leads me, hand still in mine, around a corner towards the small room, which overlooks the lower floor. The music fades a little as the hallway narrows to a small space between Declan's office and the wall. Xander doesn't knock, but yanks down the door handle and marches straight in.

In the small room, a man sits behind a mahogany desk, a tumbler glass containing brown liquid beside him as he sorts through papers. A window looks down onto the club below, and the space in the room is taken up by boxes stacked around. Declan's older than us, dressed in a cheap suit. Is he fae too? His impassive face doesn't match the perfect fae features, and although his short hair's white, there's no violet tinge to his eyes. Human.

"I thought you might turn up tonight after what happened to the fae," he sighs. "What do you want?"

"We're looking for some people and need to know if you've seen anyone different around."

Declan picks up his glass and swirls the contents. "Not a social visit then?" He cranes his head to look at me. "Are you dating?" The mocking edge to his voice riles me, and Xander drops my hand as if he's a little boy caught holding a girl's hand. "But why bring the chick in here? Who is she?"

"She's helping me out."

A short laugh erupts from Declan. "Sure, Xander. I bet she's very *helpful*."

"Yeah. She's more fun to hang out with than the guys, if you know what I mean."

Excuse me? I open my mouth to tell them I have a bloody name and I'm not his piece of ass, but Xander shoots me a look.

"Yeah, I bet she is," says the guy and stares at my breasts. I glare. "The Horsemen asking for human help? Things are slipping."

Xander ignores him and walks to the edge of the room, where glasses and a bottle of clear liquid rest on a small round table. "I'll fix us a drink, since you're not offering."

He hands me a glass; I shake my head, but Xander pushes it closer.

I'd intended to avoid alcohol, but here I am with peer pressure from a Horseman? Ha ha.

The liquid burns my throat as I drink, and I fight coughing. The man gestures for me to sit in an upholstered chair nearby, but I remain close to the door. Xander sits opposite him.

"Have you seen any demons around here recently?"

"Nope. We had a couple of vamps the other week, but they were with their donors so they didn't cause any trouble. They're allowed, right? Good paying customers."

Xander spins his glass on the desk. "You know the answer to that question, but I'll ignore what you told me as long as there're none here tonight. Anyone else suspicious?"

"Not that I'm aware of."

Xander's line of questioning continues. "Do you know anything at all about who's behind the attack on the fae queen?"

He scowls. "Hey, I'm just a guy making a living here. I don't get involved in fae business, and you guys kick my ass if a demon even sniffs in this direction."

Xander pulls his phone from a pocket and clicks, before turning the screen to Declan. "Have you seen this guy around?"

Declan takes the phone and peers at Hunter's picture. "Dunno. He's not exactly unusual looking."

Xander flicks a finger across the screen. "Might've been with this girl."

Again, Declan studies. "Oh, yeah, seen her around with friends. She's old enough, okay? We checked her ID. Friendly girl."

"This is Elyssia. Did you know she's the fae queen's daughter?"

"What the fuck? Does Arlo know?"

"Good question," says Xander. "But this is where Elyssia met the guy I showed you, the one who tried to kill her mother."

Declan holds his hands up, palms outwards. "Seriously, man, I had no clue."

"You didn't see the two together? Or with others?"

"You know I spend most evenings up here. Arlo's the one to ask."

"Where is he?"

He jerks a thumb in the window's direction. "Down there. He's checking out the clientele, as usual."

"For demons?" asks Xander.

Declan snorts. "For ass."

Xander stands. "And demons I hope."

"Seriously, man, I haven't seen any for weeks."

"Not ones you'd recognise. You know a few can glamour themselves."

Declan shuffles with papers on his desk and looks down. "Okay. Cards on the table. We've had a group of young succubi and incubi sneak in, but they fought the vamps, so we kicked them all out. The two groups can settle things between themselves. If they don't, victims never die on the premises so that's really not my problem." He nods at me. "Look, I don't know who your friend is, but I really don't like having this conversation with her around."

"And I don't like your attitude to human life," Xander growls.

"Tough. Do your job and don't expect us to do it for you. Protecting people is your job. Are you losing your touch, Xander?"

Xander places both hands on the table and leans closer. "Do you want to see if I'm losing my touch?" he says in a tone that lifts hairs on my neck. "Maybe I can bring my brother in here and see if we've lost our touch?"

Declan shrinks away. "Calm down. Jesus man, stressed much?"

"Why aren't you stressed?" sneers Xander. "Do you think if the demons are attacking fae that you're safe? That your job and life are free from their interference?" The man blinks. "If someone's trying to recruit fae, I doubt the demons will be kind to those who don't cooperate."

Declan stands and jabs a finger at Xander. "Look, we put up with you and your mates' superior attitudes, at you coming in here and inspecting us like you're some kind of mafia, but don't threaten me."

"Wake up. You're completely blinkered if you think growing demon numbers won't affect you."

"You want me to call Arlo up here and have him listen to your threats?"

"Go ahead, saves me looking for him," snarls Xander. "Someone is hiding secrets, and I won't stand for that shit!"

As the tension grows in the room, I sip the strong liquid. War at his finest shifting from diplomacy to aggression in a blink of an eye. This isn't smart.

"Xander," I step forward and touch his arm. "Let's go. He doesn't have any information to help."

Xander turns his head, with a confused expression, palms still on the table. "I'm dealing with this."

"You promised if I came with you, we'd have some fun."

"I said I'm busy."

"Then I'll need to find somebody else to spend my evening with."

Despite the fact I want to glare, I practice a coy smile, one that Declan can see me giving the guy he presumes is my hook up. If only Declan could see the dark look on Xander's.

The standoff continues and Declan looks on in amusement. "Nobody makes demands of Xander, honey. You won't last the evening."

THE FOUR HORSEMEN: BOUND

"I know Xander would do whatever I asked," I say, turning up the coy.

I gleefully take on the role, especially as Xander's discomfort grows at my behaviour. I sidle over and slap down my temptation to slide a hand across his ass. *Well, he introduced me as a hook-up.* Instead, I tug one of his hands from the desk.

"Come on, I want some Xander time."

Both men stare at me, Declan in amusement and Xander in quiet shock, but the atmosphere in the room calms.

"Fine, I'll find Arlo and get answers from him," mutters Xander. He moves back from the desk and pulls his hand from mine. "And Declan is right. Nobody ever tells me what to do, sweetheart."

With a tiny smile Xander can't see, I step out of the door in front of him.

I think he'll find I just did.

The moment the door closes, Xander grabs my arm and pulls me to one side. The space between the office and the wall is narrow, the hallway hidden and dark, away from the loud music. "What the fuck was that performance?"

"You were getting aggressive. I was trying to diffuse the situation. Worked, didn't it?"

"I have a fucking job to do. I gave him a chance to cooperate."

I place my hand on Xander's shoulder. "A chance? Is that what you call that? Why are you like this all the time?"

He gestures at himself. "War?"

"But behaving like this isn't helpful, surely? You should relax more."

"Based on your behaviour in there, I'd say you were the one who wanted to help me relax." He lowers his voice.

"You were the one implying I'm your hook up for the night. I just played along to solve a problem."

Xander places both hands above me on the wall, blocking my view with his large frame. He's close, not touching, but my body jumps to alert at his proximity and his switch from aggressive to this.

"I know the effect I have on you, Vee," he whispers. "I thought that performance might be because you want to indulge your delusion. The one where you think I want you as much as the other three do."

"And I know right now you want to show me the effect I have on you," I whisper back.

He shifts closer and trails a finger along my cheek. "They're following you around like puppy dogs, waiting for you to click your fingers. Not me."

"Is that so?"

"Yes. I wonder who you'll choose."

I laugh in his face. "Who says I'm going to choose one of you? I could take you all."

I don't know where the words come from, or if I could ever act on them, but a girl could get used to the idea four men all worship her. Yes, four, because this one's lying to my face.

"And maybe once you've had a taste of each of us, you'll choose the one who makes you scream the loudest."

Xander closes the gap between us, the intensity

growing where our bodies touch. He runs his fingers along my leg before resting his hand against my hip. "Who've you had a taste of already? My brother, yes. Joss? Surely not Ewan." Xander shifts, lips close enough to mine that his breath strokes my mouth. "Do you want a taste of me next?"

My body screams yes. Taste Xander's lips, push my hands beneath his shirt, and dig fingers into his taut muscle. I have the power to bring this arrogant man to his knees, and the idea shivers desire through my body.

I hold my head still, refusing to be drawn into my pulse-racing need to connect our mouths. If Xander's lips touch mine, the building sexual energy between us will unleash and change everything.

No.

After what happened with Heath the other night, this is a bad idea.

There's something in the air here; people dance and touch; mingled scents trigger the primal human needs. Amongst that atmosphere, I stand with Xander, predestined to react to each other in this way without even touching. But he *is* touching. I close my eyes and hold my breath against the sensory overload. I've never had the time of day for guys as arrogantly self-assured as Xander, and bond or no bond, I won't change my attitude.

"I'm not going to do anything here, Xander, so you may as well step back." My lips don't touch his as we talk, but the buzz between them builds an ache I don't want. "Please take your hands off me."

"You sure? I won't offer again."

"I'll try to deal with the disappointment," I say sarcastically.

Xander pushes himself from the wall and runs a hand across his short hair. "Cool. I'll find someone else tonight. That's never difficult."

"If that's your intention, then why try this with me? Looking for a challenge?"

He snorts. "I'm not really interested in you; I just want to piss my brother off."

My mouth parts in disgust at his amused look, but he doesn't fool me. "Is that true, Xander? There's no other reason you're this close to me right now?"

Again we stand off, eyes fixed on each other, hidden but open.

"I don't have to answer your questions, Vee."

Stepping forward, I tiptoe and place my lips close to his ear. "I think you just did, Xander."

6

EWAN

I let the world stream by as I weave along the country roads, speeding around the bends and enjoying the power this gives me. A drier day makes a long ride possible after rainy days and shit road conditions; I'm not heading after Xander just yet.

I don't have a lot of freedom, from the guys or my role, but when I ride my bike, I'm on the verge between control and the bike controlling me. My life wavers between safety and danger, but this time the split second between triumph and disaster is in my hands.

And I need more.

I skirt around the town Xander and Vee head to and back into the countryside. They'll be fine for another hour; there's no evidence trouble will join us tonight. This is just a fishing mission.

My head clears too, blowing away the stress. My loud mouth ruined the relationship with Vee. I have no clue what to say to her about the way she discovered her truth was lies. Joss told me she's okay, doesn't blame me, but he doesn't get it. I spend life hurting those who deserve pain; killing them painfully from the inside. Vee doesn't deserve her life to be eaten away the way theirs is.

She doesn't deserve pain.

I stay in the house more than the other guys, away from the constant conflict between us. I'm happy alone with my laptop and research, and this fulfills me as much as when I use my other powers to stop evil. Danger follows the Horsemen everywhere, and I like space away from that shit.

But things have stepped up; this new shit with Vee and with Portia, the demon interference, all worry me. These reminders why I'm out tonight encroach, and I turn back to the town, slowing as I reach the centre. My bike draws attention from the kids hanging around the statue in the main square as I pass, and I can't resist a rev or two for them, as I increase my speed again.

Man, I fucking love my bike.

I locate Xander's car, tucked at the industrial estate's rear, between shipping containers, and park mine beside. Isn't this too far from the club? What if we need to move fast? We can run, but Vee's not exactly dressed for an Olympic-style sprint.

Nobody stops me as I walk inside. The fae doorman informs me Xander and his chick are inside with Declan, and irritation prickles. *His chick?* Has something happened between them?

I adjust my eyes to the light, and the familiar

Warehouse dry ice and sweat smell assaults me. Of the Four, I love this place the most. I'm at home and draw little attention from humans. The tall scruffy guy with tattoos and bulk nobody wants to mess with? Yep. Perfect.

The regulars recognise me though; I've spent "intimate moments" with some girls here. This place is somewhere we come back to regularly between hunts, and because I'm away "working" for weeks on end, no girl expects more than a night. The other guys indulge too, but down time becomes less and less as we're away more.

This isn't down time, although Xander will likely use the opportunity. He's wound tight after his time away, and his getting laid will do us all a favour.

I stride towards Declan's office and halt. Looks like Xander's already started the process. He's close to the office, even closer to the person he's looking down on. His hands aren't on the girl he obscures from my view, but this man doesn't need to use his hands, silver-tongued bastard.

I blow air into my cheeks. *Jesus, man, we have a job to do.*

Xander moves to one side and my chest tightens, shooting unwarranted anger into my blood.

Vee.

Five minutes alone with her, and Xander's already persuaded Vee to get up close and personal?

Fucking hypocrite.

I stride over until I'm close enough to gauge their faces for hints of what happened between them. Xander looks at me impassively, and Vee's clothes look untouched.

"You're late," says Xander.

"Looks like I *am* late to the party." I raise a brow. Still no reaction.

"Declan has nothing to report, but Arlo is here tonight. I want to catch up with him before he leaves."

"Arlo? Where?" I ask.

"Down there, apparently." Xander points over the balcony.

I crane my head but locating anybody in there is impossible—one writhing mass, faces occasionally caught in the strobe lights. Yeah, getting up close and personal's never a problem in this place, for anybody.

Vee walks between us as we negotiate the winding steel stairs to the main floor. She stumbles as her heel's caught between the steps and I steady her. Xander moves too quickly once we reach the ground floor, and she's exposed to the crowds around her. My protective side takes hold as a guy, face covered in piercings, spiked red hair steps in front, dancing and beckoning her into the crowd.

How will Vee react to this type of treatment? I know how I will. I stride forward and step between them. Vee bumps into my back as I stare down the metal-covered dude.

"Sorry, man!" he calls and turns to a girl beside him, who has no issue with letting him wind his arms around her waist.

I step to one side and Vee resumes her path through the crowd, in the direction of Xander and the bar. I resist my instinct to put a hand on Vee, to broadcast a signal she's with me to anybody tempted to touch her. But I have no right myself. Besides, her appearance already sets fire to a need that should remain at a smoulder, and touching Vee wouldn't be a good idea.

Xander rests against the bar and clicks his fingers at the bored-looking barman. Two beer bottles appear in front of him and he leans in to ask Vee something. A few moments later, the barman places a coke beside the beers.

I rest against the bar, elbows behind, and watch the people around. Vee sips her coke, wide-eyed, but Xander appears oblivious to her discomfort.

"Have you seen Arlo?" I shout at Xander.

He shakes his head and drinks.

"What does he look like?" asks Vee.

"Very tall, skinny, white hair streaked with purple. Can't miss him."

"What? Even amongst this crowd?" she asks and her laughter sounds over the music. Then she straightens and points behind me.

I look over and see Arlo moving through the crowd. Dancers part as he passes, most not registering him. The guy's weird looking to them, but he's normal looking for a fae. I wrinkle my nose at his usual outlandish outfit. Tonight he wears tight, white trousers and a silver vest exposing his wiry muscles and tattoos. Neon eye make-up and lipstick accentuate his unorthodox look, and hide his fae side further.

Arlo's eyes fix on us as he approaches, and the light bouncing from his pale face highlights that he's unamused.

He stops short and tips his head upwards, looking down his narrow nose at us. We're the same height so he has trouble with this. To humans, this guy appears to be in his twenties. In reality, Arlo's well over a hundred. As one of the original "migrants" to the human world as a child, he's unhappy with fae politics and long since immersed himself away from their society's traditional side. He's loyal to his kind, but he won't yield his life to control by royalty.

Arlo's magic's strong so he's left to his own devices for fear he'll attempt to interfere. Involvement in the Portia plot crossed my mind, but the guy's too comfortable in this life to tip the balance and threaten his existence.

We had issues early on with Arlo allowing supernatural clientele into the club. They paid him well and, at first, Arlo denied to us that they attended. We caught him out the day we found a vamp and non-donor hidden away in a side room. Since then, we visit regularly, as much to keep tabs on whether demons moved into the area and need clearing up. Occasionally stray, younger vamps wander in unaware we'll report them to their Houses for being here.

Shifters are fine to come if they're with pack members, when grouped they never touch humans in a way that could damage or kill them. Other fae can be problematic. The younger kids enjoy living side by side with humans, whereas the elders worry they'll attract attention and prefer they don't. Less come here recently; there's a fae-only underground club nearby aimed at their teen vices and where weird shit goes down. The Four stay away. Not our circus, not our monkeys.

"This is an unexpected visit," says Arlo.

"Didn't you hear about the trouble?" asks Xander.

Arlo cups his ear as if he can't hear, which he probably can't, and gestures to the edge of the bar away from the dance floor. The music's still loud here, but at least conversation is more audible.

"Trouble in Portia's kingdom?" asks Arlo and rubs long fingers across his chin.

"As if you didn't know."

"I heard something." He waves a dismissive hand.

"Drop the clueless act. All fae know. As you live in her realm, this concerns you. We want to know if you've sighted any demons in here recently."

"Me?" He gestures to himself in mock surprise

"Yes. You," says Xander.

Arlo ignores him and switches his attention to Verity. "Is this your new friend?" He holds a hand out. Vee looks at his purple painted fingernails and long fingers before taking hold. He snatches his hand back; touching her confirms what we want to hide.

"Oh, she's your missing Fifth? You found her, then?" Arlo cocks his head as he studies Vee's face. "She's very pretty."

"Did you know any of the others looking for her?" I ask.

Arlo laughs. "A lot of people look for the Truth."

I pull myself to full height and scowl down at him. "Anybody you're friendly with?"

"Me? No. I don't get involved, you know that."

I turn to Vee. "What do you think?"

Her lips purse. "He's telling the truth."

Arlo snaps his fingers. "Ah! She spots lies! Clever trick! That must make life fun between you five. Have you asked them anything interesting yet, Vee?"

"Like what?" she asks.

"Whatever you want, if they can't lie. Man, I'd give my

right arm to play games with these guys." He runs playful fingers along Xander's arm.

Xander pushes his hand away. "Look, we just need to know if there've been any unusual 'customers' here recently."

"No." His response is definitive and firm.

"What about those vamp teens who dressed up like they were from a TV show and lured girls back to the House?"

Arlo scowls. "No fucking way, once we discovered them, we reported to their Elders and they were dealt with. Do you think I want to get involved with that shit? Nope."

His eyes shine brighter and anger masks his face. Vee shifts away, closer to me. I look at her and she nods, confirming his truth.

Arlo laughs. "Your very own lie detector. That'll make life easier for you all." The appraisal he makes of Vee's body and in particular her legs irritates me. "In some ways. How does it work then?"

"How does what work?"

"Between the five of you. Do you take turns? Or all at once?"

I clench my teeth at the amused curl to his mouth. If he were human, I'd smack him in the face for rudeness, but Arlo's only asking based on his personal norms.

"Take turns doing what?" asks Vee.

Xander leans in and whispers something. Vee blinks rapidly then looks at the ground. *Now* I want to punch him.

"We're all friends," I say. "Like family."

Arlo crosses his arms, mouth tipping up at one side. "Sure, Ewan. I wonder how long that will last?"

I bristle again and look to Xander, who pulls out his phone and shows Arlo the images of Hunter. Vee's eyes remain on the ground, and now she's frowning.

"You okay?" I ask and touch her arm.

She snaps back to reality and tiptoes to reach my ear. "I'm going to the bathroom," she says and her hair and breath brush my skin.

Vee's scent lingers, clouding my mind, as she heads towards the open hallway opposite where we stand.

7

Vee

In my old life, I'd never come to a place like this. On the rare nights out I spent with Clone Club, we visited brighter lit, bigger places filled with shiny, happy people.

Not a freak show like here.

Hypocritical of me, I know, considering what I am. And odder still, these people scare me. Can the guys detect if any are demons too? Their continued vagueness and protection begins to piss me off. Aren't I their equal?

I definitely can't detect demons, although I recognised Arlo as fae. His similarity to the guy who attacked me set hairs on my neck, but I can't fear everybody of his race based on one event. Bloody rude comment though. Sure, I've pictured more than one of the guys naked but certainly not all five of us together.

Omigod, no way. Hell, what would a girl do with so many...uh, appendages? I haven't watched enough porn to know the answer to that one, and I don't think I want to know.

The queue stretches out of the bathroom door, and I rest against the black painted wall to wait and duck as a ripped poster attacks my head. The brighter area highlights people's unfriendly faces more clearly than the gloomy club, and I keep my eyes to the floor, something I've spent a lot of time doing since I arrived here.

Ten minutes later, I emerge from the bathrooms having paddled in water and attempted to wash my hands in a sink blocked by paper towels.

So far, I'm unimpressed by my introduction to the fun Horsemen have when hunting. I wish I'd stayed home. Seriously.

The hallway's crammed with more bodies, some passing between the dance floor and bathrooms, the others queuing for or leaving the bathrooms.

A guy, similar height to me, stocky, catches my eye as I pass. His vibrant green hair's spiked, chains hanging from his leather pants. Seconds later, he bumps me sideways and I'm trapped between him and the wall as a hand slides around to my ass.

"What the fuck?" I shout and shove at his hand.

He leers at me and runs a pierced tongue along his lips. "Hey, beautiful."

His voice slurs, eyes awash with alcohol and my anger rises. "Get the hell off me!"

I'm about to bring my knee firmly into his crotch when he stumbles backwards, dragged by the shirt.

"Hey, man. I don't think you should do that." I watch as a taller, slimmer man looks down at my assailant.

The green-haired guy shoves him in the chest, but the other grabs his wrist. The second guy may look as if he has less strength, but the bigger man yelps in pain as the guy twists his arm round.

"I said, you shouldn't do that."

Others in the hallway glance at us and then away again, as if the occurrence isn't unusual. The stocky man drops his challenge, then stumbles away, muttering and rubbing his arm.

"Thanks," I say as I pull myself away from the wall.

"No problem. You okay?" He smiles down at me. He's blond, piercing-free, and the most ordinary person I've met in here.

"I'm fine." I shift my eyes in the direction of the bar, desperate to head back to Xander and Ewan.

"I haven't seen you in here before."

Oh great, he's hitting on me too.

"First time," I say brightly and sidestep a passer-by.

"On your own?"

"With some friends."

The man nods. At least his gaze remains on my face and doesn't wander elsewhere. "Having fun?"

"Uh—"

"Oh, look at me with all my questions!" He laughs. "Sorry. I'm Danny."

"Hi. Vee."

"Vee? Cool name. Short for something? Veronica? Violet?"

I shake my head again. Without Xander and Ewan close, I'm uncomfortable sharing who I am. "Just Vee."

Someone behind Danny knocks into him, and he holds out a hand, arm outstretched as he touches mine. This innocent gesture disturbs me because his touch lingers on my bare skin longer than it should. I look down at his fingers and frown. Danny slides them along my arm, and his face changes, eyes darkening as he does.

Call me paranoid (plenty do) but following the last few days, people behaving strangely bothers me.

"Sorry. I was pushed into you and your skin's very soft I couldn't resist stroking," he says, voice soft.

Uh oh. Creeper. This is worse than the guy pinning me to the wall. I stare back into his friendly eyes, which now show more interest in me than I'd like. *Oh, for fucks sake...* I'd rather deal with a mob of demons than people like him. They'd probably make my skin crawl less.

Before he can touch or talk to me again, I push my way passed a couple of girls, who're heading towards the bathrooms, and back to the bar. I look down at my arm. A small red mark appeared on my inner arm where he touched me, and I rub at the spot, which feels warm against my fingers.

Ewan and Xander are in the same spot, but Arlo's no longer with them. Ewan pushes hair from his face as he looks at me.

"Are you okay?"

"No." *Damn.* I can avoid answering direct questions if I concentrate, but at times like these, I'm caught off-guard.

Ewan moves closer, creating a block between me and those around. "What's wrong?"

"This place is full of weirdos. Two guys touched me up on the way back here."

He pulls himself to full height and glances around. "Who? Where?"

"God knows, the place is packed, they've probably moved on elsewhere by now. Hit on some other lucky girl."

"That's it. You don't go anywhere else in here on your own."

I smile at his concern. "I'm okay. I don't need protecting, I can look after myself."

Xander glances over from where he's drinking and resting against the bar. "What's going on?"

"Some dudes groped Vee."

"I'm fine," I say as Xander's brow tugs down too.

He gives a curt nod to Ewan. "Stop looking at Vee as if she's an ordinary human chick fending off guys. I'm pretty sure Vee can look after herself."

"It's not the human guys who worry me. She isn't used to dealing with demons yet."

Xander drains his bottle and wipes his mouth with the back of a hand. "Okay. Fine. I don't care what Arlo says, I swear there're demons in here tonight. We can practice your new powers on them. Right, Vee?"

I nod, wishing my confidence in using my unknown powers matched Xander's. With the movement, a wooziness comes over me, my vision blurring for a second, and I blink it away before either guy notices my slight sway.

I should've eaten before drinking.

The sensation washes again, and I grip the edge of the bar.

Thankfully Ewan's and Xander's attention is elsewhere, and neither see. I pull in a breath. The heat and claustrophobia in here doesn't help the intoxication.

"How long are we staying?" I ask.

"Xander wants to hang around even if we don't find any demons," says Ewan and inclines his head.

A girl serving behind the bar leans on the counter, breasts swelling against her tight blue vest top as she bends forward to talk to him. Xander's interest is plain as he winds a finger around her long blonde hair and gives a smile guaranteed to charm any girl.

Ewan shoves him in the shoulder. "Oi, Romeo! We haven't finished yet. Didn't you just say we needed to look around?"

Xander whispers something to the girl who nods and looks at him from under her lashes. He joins us. "We'll scout around the rest of the place, and if Arlo's right and there's no one here who shouldn't be, you can head home. I'm hanging here for a while in case the situation changes."

"Oh yeah? So we'll see you in the morning, huh?" Ewan pulls his mouth into a knowing smile.

"Maybe." Xander indicates the girl with his head. "That's up to her. Come on, we have a better view of everyone if we head upstairs to the balcony. Another?" He gestures at the empty bottles.

Ewan shakes his head. "We're driving, remember?"

"I won't be. Not until tomorrow." He winks. "Vee? Drink?"

I shake my head. A mistake as the surroundings remain shaky once I stop. I stare at Ewan as he speaks to Xander. Holy crap, the man's hot. He's removed his jacket, and taut biceps emerge from the T-shirt sleeves. There's a raw power to Ewan he could play up if he wanted, and his lack of arrogance is more attractive to me than Xander's attitude. The barrier that this brooding guy hides behind makes him oh so much sexier.

That and his killer body.

I imagine how he'd touch me. Ewan wouldn't be gentle; he'd know what he wants and would overwhelm me. I moisten my lips as he turns, and a sudden, intense sexual need flows through as he meets my eyes.

I swear I'm an ounce of self-control from pushing myself against him, grabbing his hair, and kissing the hell out of him. Right here. Right now.

I blink. What is wrong with me?

Ewan looks away quickly, and I do too. How obvious was my intent?

"Come on. Upstairs." Oblivious, Xander takes a beer he ordered from the bar and ploughs into the dancers. Ewan follows and reaches behind to take my hand.

His touch explodes fireworks beneath my skin, stronger than any reaction to the other three guys. I stumble after him, body lit up as if someone spent the last ten minutes focusing on my arousal.

Hell, I want somebody to spend the next ten minutes focused on my body.

I want Ewan.

What is this? I drop Ewan's hand, worried about my next reaction to the effect he has, and continue to follow. The crowd swells between us, moving in unison to the music, side to side, and jostling. I focus on following Ewan's head visible above the people, but when a guy as tall as Ewan steps in front of me, I lose sight of him.

Shit.

The disorientation hits again. Hands pull me into the throng, and the room spins as faces fade in and out of view. I stumble around, confused by the world lurching from side to side. I need to find Ewan and Xander.

I push in the direction of the stairs, craning my neck to try to spot their tall figures on the balcony.

"Vee."

Somebody grabs my hand again, and I'm about to snatch my fingers away when I look into Ewan's face.

"I thought I'd lost you!" I shout over the music.

Ewan inclines his head toward the stairs and pulls me after him. We don't reach them; instead he veers to the right and pulls me into the shadows at the edge of the dance floor.

"Everything okay?" I ask.

Ewan places a hand in the small of my back and pulls me to him. Hard lips hit mine, knocking my breath away in surprise. He pulls me closer still, fingers splaying across my back as he cradles my head with his other hand. My desire takes over as I return his kiss, lacing my fingers into his hair and holding his face to mine. I was right. There's nothing gentle about Ewan's passion as he parts my mouth with his tongue, and deepens the kiss.

This is different to kissing Heath, as none of Ewan's memories appear in my mind, and the link remains purely physical. I'm engulfed by need, but not by a need to connect. Am I disappointed I wanted to feel more with Ewan? That maybe Heath's right and something different exists between me and each guy? Right now, hell no because any man who can trigger the building explosion inside with just a kiss is the one I want.

People either side jostle us, but I barely notice,

oblivious to anything but Ewan. I wrench my mouth away, desperate for air.

Ewan looks up, towards the balcony where Xander headed. "Not here," he calls in my ear.

Arm around my waist, Ewan guides me back in the direction where I stood at the bar with the two guys earlier. Insanity follows me along a narrow hallway and into a small room towards the building's rear, containing a blue fabric sofa and a table strewn with empty glasses and fast food wrappers. I catch sight of a staff roster on the wall before my view's obliterated by Ewan as he seizes my face and kisses me again.

The heat between us, the intoxicating scent from his skin, and the strength in the shoulders I grip onto consume me, as the urgency continues. A dizziness matching earlier by the bar washes over me. My body fills with exhaustion, the new kiss pulling me towards unconsciousness. This contradiction makes no sense, but my body and brain shut down as I disconnect from reality. Legs buckling, I fall backwards onto the sofa. I fight to keep my eyes open as Ewan stands over me, lust filling his hooded eyes, but the dizzy dark consumes.

8

EWAN

I stand on the balcony overlooking the dance floor, snapping my head between watching people on the stairs and scouring the crowd for Vee.

"Where the hell is she?" I growl at Xander.

"Hey, don't get pissy with me. You were the one who lost her."

Lost her. "Fuck you."

"Whoa, calm down. She'll be fine."

"How do you know that? She said some guy came onto her. What if —"

"Come on, this place may be filled with freaks, but the place is too busy for a girl to be dragged screaming through the club. Especially not her. Vee might not have control over her powers, but something that threatens her will trigger them."

I want to believe his words, but something doesn't feel right here. The way she looked at me before we headed away from the bar and over here blew me away. She seriously looked as if she were about to tear my clothes off. Our relationship hit awkward since the "big reveal" fuck up, and there's no way either of us are near to acting on the tension between us.

"I'm going to look for Vee. What if those we're trying to find have found her first?" I rub a palm across my mouth. "We're not immune to every trick a demon can pull, especially any that influences our human side."

Xander's not listening. He grips my arm and points into the sea of sweaty black below.

"Do you see what I see?" he asks.

I peer through the dim. Lost in the crowd's midst, two women surround a guy, one kissing him and the other behind, sliding her hands down the front of his jeans.

"Yeah. A guy getting very lucky," I reply.

"No, dumbass. They're holding him up. Look at his arms loose by his side."

I peer closer. He's right. "Shit. Demons?"

"Yeah, succubi. I bet there's a fucking gang of them around."

"But they're attacking him in front of everybody!"

Xander shakes his head and places his bottle on the nearby table. "Like that matters. Half the people dancing are practically screwing each other."

I rake a hand through my hair, momentarily forgetting about Vee as I know the man's life's in danger. "When did they arrive?"

"Unless we come face to face, it's hard to spot them."

"Should've brought Joss," I mutter.

"No. We both know he's best suited to scouting out demons' nests and we need to work separately to cover all angles."

"Yeah, and we need to stop *them*!" I jab a finger in the direction of the two girls. "Then we need serious words with Arlo about this."

"Maybe he doesn't know."

"Sure." I snort.

We take the steps two at a time as we charge down them. Two succubi sharing the same guy means there's a real possibility they'll kill him. The demons must be young, because public attacks like this are a dumb idea. On top of that, sharing him increases the chance they'll drain the guy's energy too quickly. He'll die in public. In the club.

Yeah, they're either young or dumb, or both.

If the attack happened outside, this would be easier for us: a quick dispatch with a knife. But here, we'd draw attention however subtly we can kill following years of practice. I nod at Xander who approaches the girl kissing the guy and drags her backwards. Black hair falls down the succubi's back as she tips her head to look at Xander, eyes lazy with pleasure, and touches his face.

Xander spins her around so her back's against his chest. She doesn't struggle, instead continuing to move to the music, arms behind her, running hands along Xander's legs as she rubs herself against him.

One advantage we have is not all demons know what the Horsemen look like, or can detect who we are. Of course, those higher up their food chain, the ones attempting to interfere with our work, would spot us from across a room. They follow our moves, send lower caste demons after us, but these girls are different. Renegade. Young. Focused on their own lives while waiting for the day their demon superiors bring the world to its knees.

Have they any idea who we are?

The girl holding the guy drops her hold from around his waist and terror crosses her face. I guess that answers my question. I catch the guy as he slumps into my arms, his tall figure heavy with semi-consciousness.

"It's the fucking Horsemen!" she yells at her friend. The succubi darts into the crowd leaving the other girl firmly in Xander's grip. With the guy in my arms I'm unable to follow.

Another girl dancing alongside us gives a curious look. I pull a face at her and smile in an attempt to communicate I'm helping a drunk friend. Simultaneously, the girl in Xander's arms stops dancing and attempts to pull away, digging nails into his grip on her waist.

We drag the demon and victim into a quieter corner before anybody else notices what's happening. Ironically, we look like two guys assaulting a girl, and that can cause more problems than the one we're about to fix. Fortunately, club security know who we are and never bother with us.

"Is he alive?" asks Xander above the music.

The man shifts against me and mumbles, answering Xander's question.

The girl whimpers as Xander takes hold of her shoulders and shakes. "How many of you are here?"

She gives up on her escape attempt, the high from her victim's energy soothing the fear she should have. She waves a hand around. "Me, her, a couple of guys from our family."

"Incubi too? Are you fucking insane? Anybody who crosses into this place to feed risks death if we're around," shouts Xander over the music.

"He invited us!" She indicates the guy now sitting on the floor. "He's a friend."

"A friend you're sucking the life out of?" I snap.

"Well, he thinks we're friends, since we happen to look like the two chicks he's spent months lusting after." Her beautiful face curves into a smile. "We didn't need to use magic to turn this one on."

Fear trickles down my spine like ice. They've glamoured themselves to look like people he knows? These scum often disguise themselves with magic, and use the same power to switch off everything in a victim's brain apart from sexual arousal. One touch and the victim's infected the way I'll happily infect this *thing* with my own brand of magic.

Fuck. What about the guys who groped Vee?

No, I'm being paranoid. Any guy could've touched Vee; she's an attractive girl and plenty would grab the opportunity to put their hands on her.

Surely Vee would notice if they were supernatural.

But would she? This incubus's appearance is as human as the girl dancing nearby. *We* can't always detect demons, and we've had years of practice.

Shit.

I flashback to Vee rubbing her arm. Did they mark her and infuse magic into her body? The ice chills my blood further. I really fucking need to find her.

I drop the guy who slumps against the wall, head lolling to one side. "You sort this. I need to find Vee."

I don't wait for Xander's inevitable protest.

The paranoia intensifies as I plunge back into the dancing bodies, searching for any sign of Vee. I shove at those blocking my path, staring down any guys who take offence and challenge me. I know my way around this club, spent evening after evening involved in searches like this, but for demons not the girl who means the world to all of us. I kick open doors to rooms as I pass along the hallway leading to the rear of the building.

Nothing.

The last room I come to is locked. Not caring or waiting, I step back and slam my foot into the black door as hard as I can. The lock splinters and door flies open.

The scene greeting me triggers a rage I've never experienced before. The individual standing with his back to me a few feet away is about to experience my rage too, and it won't be pretty.

Vee's lying on the sofa unconscious, head hanging off the edge and hair falling towards the floor. A guy stands over her and he twists his head around at the noise caused by my kicking down the door. His brown eyes widen in surprise, but he's not as fucking surprised as I am. I stare back at the man who matches my height, build, *face*.... my mirror image.

What the fuck?

The space around him shimmers; the guy's body and face change to reveal someone completely different. As he transforms, his brown curls switch for blond hair, and he becomes slimmer. *A glamour.* I was fucking right; this guy's an incubus who's preying on Vee.

I flick my eyes to Vee. Her clothes are intact, but what the hell would've happened if I hadn't arrived?

"You fucking demon bastard!" I yell, and in seconds he's on the floor, beneath me with my knees on his chest.

Tonight he can be the victim pinned down and killed.

"Get the fuck of me!" he snarls, but realisation who I am dawns across his face now we're closer. "Shit."

"Oh yeah, shit." I pull back a fist and bone crunches as I smack him in the face. "Do you know who that is you're about to rape and kill?" I snarl.

"Rape? She's consenting and fucking desperate to screw you," he sneers.

My hand's back, ready to strike again, but I pause at his words.

"You know how we operate, Horseman. You saw me; I glamoured myself. I lifted the image of a guy from her mind—one she wants to *fuck*." He pauses then silently mouths the word "you" before breaking into a grin.

No way. Blood smears his face and my knuckles as my fist collides with his broken face again. "She's not fucking consenting!"

The man rubs his stained lips together. "With a bit of magic persuasion, they're always up for a good time. Man, you should give her a go. Amazing tits, shame I never got my hands on them."

I grab his shirt, lift him forward, and slam his head on the floor with a sickening thud. He blinks back at me and laughs. Pulling him close again, his face almost touches mine.

"If she thinks you're me, and you're not, that's assault. How far have you gone with her? If you've hurt her I will kill you so slowly and painfully you'll wish you were in Hell," I spit out.

The demon chokes on the blood gathering in his mouth. "Not far enough, thanks to you. Just a kiss or two. She lost consciousness before we could get down to the good stuff."

A lot in my life pisses me off; I've witnessed some evil shit by demons before but never to somebody close to me. This? Livid doesn't even begin to describe the rage consuming each and every cell in my body.

I grip the incubus's neck with both hands and he gasps. Veins in his neck blacken, and the blackness moves upwards and across his disfigured face. The disease and decay I infuse with my fingers continues its deadly journey through his body, and his eyes redden as the blood vessels burst.

"The girl you're assaulting? She's our Fifth. If she'd known who you were you'd be fucking dead already."

He gasps a laugh. "I think she wanted to believe I was you."

No. No. *No.* I squeeze my anger into his neck.

The demon retches as the disease takes hold, fluid filling his lungs and I keep my grip on him while I grasp at what the hell is happening here. Xander's right. Vee needs to learn to defend herself until she grows into the strength we presumed she could summon.

A movement from the sofa catches my eye as Vee sits and props herself on one arm. She stares, pale face marred by shock, and touches her mouth with shaking fingers.

"Ewan. What are you doing?" Her eyes flick to the dying demon. "Who's that?"

"The demon you thought was me," I snarl. I shake him again. "Isn't that right?"

The guy turns his head to look at Vee, blood caking his face. "Don't you recognise me, sweetheart?"

She continues to touch her lips. "He was one of the guys who came on to me. The one who touched me. Why is he in here with us?"

"The bastard glamoured himself to look like me," I bark out. "He'd already magiced you into a state of uh... arousal. I just arrived. He was the one who brought you in here, not me." I meet Vee's eyes and wait for the truth to catch up.

"Omigod." Vee tears her gaze from mine and slumps back down again. She rakes hands into her hair. "He's the one I kissed?"

"Yes," rasps the demon with a laugh. "We could've had so much fun if your friend hadn't interrupted."

The demon bastard doesn't laugh for much longer as the blackened veins burst sending a putrid darkness across his skin and choke the remaining life from him. His body slackens, and I drop the evil creature's neck. I wish I'd prolonged his death, but I want this over and to get Vee the hell out of here.

I rest back on my haunches and look to Vee. "I'd ask if you were okay but guess that's a bloody stupid question."

She chews on a nail, eyes hard and not glistening with the tears I'd expect. "Don't tell anybody what happened."

"That's your biggest worry here?" I ask. "That the others would find out? Vee, a guy just assaulted you."

"He only kissed me." She glares at the body on the floor.

I blink. "That's still assault."

As I stand and then sit next to Vee on the sofa, she shifts slightly and pulls at the dress to cover more of her legs.

Realisation hits as she refuses to meet my eyes. "He wasn't me," I say. "The scum dead on the floor who touched you is—was—an incubus. Do you know what they are?"

"Sort of. I know they feed from humans, and it has something to do with sex." She swallows.

"Demons. They're male succubi who feed on unconscious females by having sex with them. The sexual energy fuels them. You're their food source."

"But how?" She grits her teeth. "Surely I'd know what he was."

I point at Vee's arm, at the smallest mark, no bigger than a thumbprint bruise. "Magic, Vee. You had no idea." She closes her shaking hand over it.

"This is bullshit, Ewan! You guys say I have special powers, yet demons can still freaking attack me?"

I recoil at her anger. Vee's breathing's shallow, cheeks pink, and she can't look at me. I ache to put arms around her and hug tight, but don't know if she wants me to.

"You can't always spot demons. It sucks, but it's true. Don't you think our job would be a hell of a lot easier if we could pick demons out more easily? We're powerful but not infallible, Vee. You didn't feel in danger or know, so nothing triggered your powers."

Her demeanour changes, and she drops her head back onto the sofa. "Fuck. I passed out. Was he... When you walked in. It was just kissing, wasn't it?"

"Yes." My stomach twists at the thought of what I could've seen, and I give in to my need, wrapping Vee in my arms and holding her close. Vee's cheek touches my chest, but her muscles remain tense, and she doesn't yield to my desperation to comfort her.

The succubus told us there were four of them altogether, which means I need to get Vee to safety, then find and subject his friend to a painful death too.

I can't help the question rattling in my brain. Why me? Why not Xander? I saw Vee with him, intimate, when I arrived, positive she wanted him. The incubus must've seen both of us in her mind. Why did Vee favour me?

I wish she bloody hadn't. Everything between us was already a mess and is now fucked up more than ever.

9

Vee

Ewan keeps his promise and doesn't say a word to Xander. He messages him and escorts me from the club, through the fire doors at the back. An alarm sounds, but Ewan strides through despite somebody appearing in the doorway to yell at us.

"I told Xander to meet us at his car," Ewan informs me and we walk across the dirty tarmac in silence.

I shake, my mind missing chunks of the last hour, and when I close my eyes, all I see is Ewan's face looking down at me, his lips on mine and hands on my body. I waver between anger over the attack and mortification I imagined the demon was Ewan. Why the hell did I?

As Xander strides towards us, he clicks the key fob and the lights flash as the Aston Martin unlocks. Ewan pulls open the car door and I slide onto the cool leather seat, not looking at him as he slams it shut behind me. I huddle down in the seat as the two guys talk.

I'm beyond grateful Ewan found me when he did, but I can't separate the incubus and him in my mind. He probably takes my inability to meet his eyes as pissed off with him, or upset by the attack, but I'm bloody embarrassed I've revealed my feelings. Ewan now knows how I see him. How can I look Ewan in the face knowing he doesn't want me, but that he knows I fantasise about him?

Minutes later, Xander climbs into the driver's seat and I eye him warily. He starts the engine.

"You're a bit of a lightweight, huh?" he says as he releases the handbrake.

"Pardon?"

"Ewan said he found you sitting in a corner having thrown up in the bathrooms. Seriously, you had one vodka, Vee."

"Must've been something I ate," I mumble. The perspiration across my back cools under the car's air con, and I shiver.

"All good. But you should've stayed with us or told us where you were going."

"I lost you in the crowd."

"Yeah, pretty crazy in there, huh?"

I clear my throat as he manoeuvres the car onto the nearby street. "I think next time you guys should go on your own."

"Not your best intro to hunting if you don't see us kill the bastards. Demons *were* in there. Found a couple of succubi, and Ewan took out one of their male counterparts before he found you. He's headed back to find the fourth in the group before he comes home."

I swallow. "Good."

Xander sighs and leans over to switch on the car radio. "I don't want to sound like a chauvinist asshole, but I think we need to teach you more skills to defend yourself. I mean, Ewan freaked when he couldn't find you, and I admit I was a bit worried too."

A muscle in his cheek twitches.

"Or maybe just teach me how to use my bloody powers!" I snap then draw in a shaky breath.

"Did something happen to you?" he asks in a low voice. "You're tense."

I breathe out, pushing away the truth ready to come out of my mouth and find vague words instead. "I had a stressful evening."

Xander huffs. "Yeah, waste of fucking time. I questioned the succubi before I killed her, and she's no idea who Portia is. No demons apart from those predators. Sure, we cleared out that gang but they're low life, a demon underclass. Their kind live for one thing only."

I dig nails into my palm. *Don't I know it.*

"I hope Joss and Heath had a better evening than us and found some clues. The longer this goes on, the worse things could get between us and the fae," he says. "I don't have time to chase around. I need names and to deal with the fucking problem."

Xander slams his foot on the accelerator and I lurch, gripping the seat.

"You didn't stay behind for your fun," I say with a

weak smile. "At least you would've achieved something for yourself."

For a moment Xander stares ahead, gripping the steering wheel tighter. "Some things are more important."

I think his pause is the end of the conversation as I stare at his hard-set jaw, but he turns his head to me. "I spent a long time looking for you, Vee, and I can't lose you." The strange intensity in his eyes matches that from before, but is as unfathomable. He looks back at the road. "Besides, it's not like you could ride home on Ewan's bike dressed like that."

His attempt to backpedal doesn't fool either of us.

Joss

Vee's distress hits my radar as soon as she walks into the lounge room. She flops on to the armchair and leans down to undo her shoes, before kicking them off and wriggling her toes. Xander heads into the kitchen to speak to Heath.

What happened? "Where's Ewan?" I ask.

"Some demons were at the club. He stayed behind because one of them disappeared." Her voice is flat. "We came home because I wasn't feeling well."

"Bad night, huh?"

"I think she had too much to drink." Xander walks passed. "I'm going to shower the demon filth off me."

His footsteps thud upstairs as I focus on Vee's face. "You don't seem drunk. Did someone try to attack you again?"

Vee abruptly stands and grabs her shoes from the floor. "I'm tired, Joss. Long night. Eye opening."

I watch in disbelief as she follows Xander upstairs. A thought crosses my mind: is she heading after him? Or avoiding me? My bedroom door opens with a familiar creak. Okay, she's not following Xander.

A weird response to me though. I put down the book I was reading and pad up the stairs after her. "Vee?" I rap on my bedroom door.

Xander appears from his adjacent bedroom, shirtless, holding a towel. He shakes his head at me. "You three are sad bastards, all desperate for her attention. Just go out and get laid, Joss."

"Shut the fuck up. Something's wrong. What happened?"

Xander shrugs. "We lost her for ten minutes or so. She was throwing up in the bathrooms, apparently."

I didn't detect any drunkenness around her. The club isn't far; she couldn't sober up this quickly. "Who found her?"

"Ewan."

"And he said nothing happened? No demons or fae approached her?"

"Ewan would've said if there'd been any problems. The girl's not used to clubs and drinking. That's all."

"And did you find any information?"

He snorts. "Nope. Wild fucking goose chase."

"Wasn't a wasted exercise if you found some renegades."

"True." He pushes down the handle on the bathroom door. "I'm getting my shower. Stay out of her bed."

"My bed," I remind him.

He shakes his head and walks into the bathroom. I knock on my door again. "Vee?"

A tired Vee opens the door and stares back at me. She's changed into flannel pyjamas with black cats on them, brushed hair framing her face. A mess of emotions emanates from her and I can't sort through which is strongest. Upset? Fear? Anger? What the fuck happened to her?

"Can I come in?" I ask.

Without speaking, Vee steps back and I close the door behind me. My room looks the same, but with her possessions spread around. The lemon scent I associate with Vee and a subtle perfume she wore tonight fill the air around.

"You look like you need a hug," I tell her and open my arms. "I guess you felt a little out of your depth tonight?"

Vee hesitates before stepping into my embrace. She doesn't hold me in return but her body gradually relaxes in my arms. I place my chin on her head, relishing the warmth but worried by the confused emotions within her. This is what I worry about: Vee might be our missing Fifth, but how strong is she? She's not one of us yet.

"Ewan and Xander should've looked after you properly."

The emotion in her switches, annoyance bubbling through, and she pulls back to look at me. "I don't need looking after. Hell, I've lived my own life without four big, bad guys looking after me."

"Wow, okay." I stroke her hair. "You gotta understand most girls we come across need rescuing."

Despite her hard look, tears reach her eyes, and she swallows. "I don't want this conversation. I had a shit night. If you want to help me, do your Joss thing."

"My Joss thing?" I itch to follow this up with the same banter as earlier, but her face warns me not to. "I'll do whatever you need," I whisper and cup her cheek. "What do you need?"

Vee's mouth so close, with her skin velvet soft beneath my fingers, and her scent surrounding us, all pull together in an intoxicating mix. My need to protect and be what Vee needs is challenged by a need of my own. Would kissing her amplify my ability to take away whatever upsets her? Or would my physical desire rush through and wipe that power away, replacing the comfort with something else? I ache for this girl, literally some days, but now I hurt because I want to show her I can be tender and loving. I want to show that my straight-down-the-line statements that I want sex with her are only part of how I feel.

I hold both Vee's cheeks with my hands and extend my arms so the intimacy drops. She looks back, pale. "Just a hug, Joss."

I do as she asks. Ewan can tell me what happened because her evasive words hide a truth. "I wish you'd tell me what's really wrong."

I'm surprised when her arms wrap around my torso. "It doesn't matter. But one things for sure, it won't happen again, and I'm ready to fight every last one of the bastards."

I detect an intense anger pushing out the fear; an inner strength greater than I expected. I'm positive she's using this to deal with whatever the hell happened tonight. My need to protect her is joined by a new realisation: I underestimated her.

We've all underestimated Vee, and I believe there's more to Truth that we still don't know.

10

Vee

My memories follow me into my dreams, confusion wrecking my head. They're vague, disturbing, the magic causing me to fade in and out of awareness. I remember his mouth on mine. His taste. Scent.

How he looked like Ewan.

I turn in bed and cover my head with a pillow, anger at the violation seeping in. I wish Ewan hadn't killed the bastard; I'd rather have ended him myself. Like many girls, I've experienced sly groping from guys conveniently close on buses, along with unwarranted comments. Once before I had a guy kiss me without consent and I rewarded him with a knee to the balls. But this...

Helpless. I don't do helpless. The guys need to show me how I can defend myself against these people who

THE FOUR HORSEMEN: BOUND

want to prey on or kill me. If my power needs working on to reach full strength, I need to protect myself in the meantime. Give me daggers, holy water, or whatever else they use, and I've no qualms about using them anymore.

Before we left the room, Ewan explained there was nothing I could've done in the situation. The incubi and succubi acted in pairs, distracting the victim so the other could use magic to induce arousal and then sleep. Only once their victim slept could they take the energy they needed by sexual assault.

Ewan told me I was lucky, and I understand what he meant but couldn't say. Lucky I wasn't raped. I shake away the thought. I don't want to run through the memories again. Can't.

The unspoken question hovered between us last night. Why did the incubus disguise himself as Ewan? I want to ask, but I know the answer. Of the two guys I spent time with last night, he's the one I fight my attraction to. I've no doubt if Heath or Joss had been present, it could easily be one of them.

But it wasn't, and now I can't look Ewan in the face.

The sun's barely risen when my sleepless night ends with a need to take in fresh air and nature to clear my mind. I step out the back door, heading for the path towards the open fields, and find Xander outside, alone, on his phone. He hastily finishes the call when he hears my feet crunch across the ground and tucks his phone away.

"You're up early for somebody who had a heavy

night," he says. "How's the hangover?"

Still wound tight from the events last night, I snap back at him. "I wasn't drunk."

"Sure." His eyes glisten with amusement. Xander's jacketless in the cool morning, a black shirt unbuttoned across a grey T-shirt, which stretches across the contours of his chest. His eyes are bright, curious even. "Where are you headed?"

"A walk," I say.

"Not far, I hope."

"Not sure."

"Want some company?"

I fold my arms across my chest. "Really?"

"Why so shocked?"

"I'm too tired for War games if that's your intention."

He grins. "No, I'm in a better mood today."

We trudge away from the house, across the field towards the woods bordering the property. My breath mists around my face, and the crisp air carries the damp earthy scent around. We don't speak, but the discomfort I expected isn't with us. I guess the desire to be around them all also applies to the guy I don't particularly like spending time with.

I wait for some snark or a reference to our encounter in the club before Ewan arrived. Was that moment between us a challenge? Or a warning? He stares ahead, hands in pockets and cheeks reddened by the cool. He's as beautiful as the other guys, but the tension around him rarely leaves. I'm confused because I secretly love the idea of meeting his challenge and seeing where things could lead.

I also like that Xander's the guy less inclined to wrap

me in cotton wool; he could solve one problem. I halt. "Can I ask you something? My power, whatever it is, can you teach me how to use it?"

Xander scrunches his face up. "You already know. You've been doing it for years—detecting lies."

"Not that, the other thing. The light."

"Ah." Xander purses his lips. "I would, but, to be completely honest with you, I don't know what your true powers are, and I can't teach you anything."

My spirits sink into my shoes. I was sure this man knew secrets the others held back, that as War he'd know how to use our individual abilities.

"But you knew I'd... explode or whatever when we were at Portia's house."

"Yeah, we know you enhance our powers, but not how. I didn't know what would happen that day, just that you would amplify my power through connecting to me. I've no idea how Heath summons the energy to kill. Or how Ewan's and Joss's powers work."

"But you felt stronger with me?"

"Oh yeah, you definitely turned my strength up a notch or ten." He grins. "Maybe the light was the energy; something inside you 'charging up'. Who the hell knows?"

"I bloody wish I did." I pause. "I felt stronger at that moment though; angrier."

"Huh. Maybe it's a two way thing and you take on some of our individual powers when we connect."

"That'd be awesome." I voice my thoughts. "All four powers. I'd wreck the world! Every last evil bastard."

Xander gives me a strange look. "You sound like you want to start with someone in particular."

"I need to learn how first."

"Yeah, not sure I can help you with that part. Sorry."

The only way to hide my frustration at his words is to walk away.

"I can teach you other things," he calls as I approach the nearby trees. "If you want."

"What things?" I turn.

"Self-defence."

"I know self-defence. I took classes."

"Against the supernatural?" he asks. "I doubt it. Their weak spots are different to humans, and from race to race."

We study each other for a moment. His attitude to me last night, the semi-proposition as we stood against the wall in the club, pissed me off, but he's the only guy not treating me with kid gloves.

"Unless they use magic," I mutter.

Xander steps forward and frowns down at me. "Did something happen? I sense something's not right; I did last night when we drove home."

I suck my lips together and wait for the "tell the truth" to pass. "Show me some self-defence moves, then."

Xander wrinkles his nose. "I dunno..."

"What? Why? Scared I'll beat you?" I retort.

"Seriously? No. I'm scared I'll hurt you."

"Try me." I beckon him with both hands. "Bring it on, Pony Boy." Portia's nickname for the boys amuses me, mostly because it clearly pissed them off. "But no knives."

In an instant, Xander lunges and seizes me, one arm around my neck. I claw at his arm but his grip tightens. I'm shocked by his sudden move and on the burn spreading through from where our bodies touch.

Again. This reaction to all four men is beyond a joke.

XANDER

Holy hell.

My body courses with an overwhelming energy, fuelled by her mocking implication she could match my combat skills. I fight down how this clouds my head because this is the reason I stay disconnected from Vee, mentally and physically. She's the centre of us all, and something not yet understood places her inside our hearts and souls too. Seizing hold of Vee has the opposite effect to what I intended; she's gained control of me by shattering the barrier I attempted to build.

Which means I focus on the task, literally, in hand to rebuild this. I push down the awareness of how soft the skin is on her arms, how her warmth fills me with heat, and forge on.

"An assailant would hold you tighter than this. Show me what you'd do."

"I'll hurt you," she says through gritted teeth and jabs an elbow upwards into my neck. I flinch as she collides with my windpipe.

"Good." I release her, and as she faces me, I'm distracted again. Why when I look into Vee's eyes, do I see something my soul craves, a missing piece I can't grasp? Mesmerised, I miss her next move, as she side steps and catches one leg around mine.

I stumble but regain my footing. What the fuck? I trap

her long leg, between my thighs. Should I throw her to the ground? Win? "Nice try, Verity."

She drags her leg away and crosses her arms. "Thanks. What next?"

I run my tongue along my teeth. Fine. "Vamps, you go here." I indicate my neck with a slicing motion. "If you have a knife, hold it horizontally against their throat and push. Head gone, dead vamp."

She blinks. "You must carry bloody sharp knives."

"They're silver. Slices through the bastards like butter."

Did she just pale? "Okay."

"Explaining what to do is harder with demons because there're so many varieties. With most, it's a simple kill—to the heart, exactly the way you would with a human. Some are stronger, but holy water in the face slows them down."

A familiar confusion purses Vee's lips. "If you have superpowers, why do you need knives?"

I give an amused snort. "Superpowers?"

"Powers that can kill, then."

"Hand to hand is quicker and easier sometimes. Draws less attention too."

I frown as laughter bubbles from Vee. "Knifing people or cutting their heads off draws less attention?"

"Demons. Not people. And yes. Look at it this way, using powers takes energy. If we use that energy up on lowlife, and harder enemies follow, we aren't at our best to fight them. Okay?" I get Vee's need to understand her new life, but her incessant questioning of what we've done for years annoys me.

"And now I'm here you have more energy."

"Precisely."

"Am I supposed to take a backpack of supplies with me everywhere?" she says, mouth twitching in amusement. "Ask them to stop their nefarious deeds while I select a weapon?"

"This isn't a joke," I growl.

"Sorry. Sarcasm is my superpower." *For fuck's sake.* She catches my annoyance. "Xander, sorry, humour is my way of dealing with this headfuck, okay?"

I huff. "Yes, we carry most in our car and take what we anticipate we'll need when we confront them." I hold my jacket to one side, revealing a knife tucked into my coat. "And I anticipate always."

Vee studies the knife. "What about the fae?"

"We don't kill them. Though my brother needs reminding about that."

"But what if they're trying to kill me? Y'know, like that guy did."

I push a hand through my hair. "Just disarm them somehow. Ask them a lot of questions. Confuse them. Whatever. Usually they have demons do their dirty work. You'll be fine. If you believe your life is under threat, I'm sure your powers will trigger."

"But magic? How do I resist that?"

"Vee, we're not invincible. We're susceptible to magic."

Her face clouds and she shakes her hands out by her sides, loosening the muscles. "Right, so I beat the hell out of everything before they get as far as magic."

I curl my mouth in amusement. "I guess you could try, but that might become problematic if you accidentally 'beat the hell' out of a human. I think you'd probably need a bit more practice first, though. You're clearly not capable of one on one, since I beat you that easily."

Her mouth thins as she stares back, chest rising and falling rapidly. I turn my back and prepare to walk away.

"Not up to it?" Vee's body hits my back as she runs at me and curls an arm around my neck. I stagger forwards due to the force, fighting to steady myself. Vee pushes her knees into the back of mine and my legs give way. This time I can't stop myself falling as I land on my hands and knees. Autumn leaves crunch beneath my palms as they hit the hard ground and fury blackens my eyes.

Who the fuck does she think she's messing with?

I stare downwards, head bowed, for a few seconds, listening to Vee's breathing above me as I anticipate her next move. She doesn't react. Is Vee worried about what she just did?

Silently, I stand and brush leaves from my knees, eyes remaining down as I watch Vee's feet to see which way she moves.

She doesn't.

Playing nice ends now, Verity. I charge at Vee, knocking her backwards. If this were one of the guys, I'd let him painfully hit the floor, but I manage to rein in enough of my temper to catch her weight before she lands. She lashes out at me, so I allow her to sink to the ground. Hair splayed above her head, Vee looks back in shock as I sit across her hips, pinning her to the damp earth.

My breath picks up, and I deny this is because my legs are either side and Vee's body's beneath me. I grip Vee's wrists in one hand and hold her arms above her head. "I'm not a demon, Vee, I'm War and the chances you'll beat me? Zero."

Challenge remains in her expression, but with wariness added as her struggle against me stops.

I hold my face closer. "What would you do in this position?"

Her hot breath touches my cool cheek. "To you? Or a demon?"

"Me."

"That's easy," she murmurs. "If I kissed you, there's no way you could hold me here. You'd lose the ability to think straight."

She moistens her lips. We're here again. I'm so close to giving in—to her and myself. Curious to see how she'll react, I close the last few millimetres between our mouths until my lips touch the edge of hers.

Wrong move. The soft buzz from the briefest touch electrifies and I jerk back, before the attempt to show my superiority backfires totally. I can't mock the other three guys when I'm as spellbound as them.

I'm right; this girl has more power over me than I'm prepared to give her.

Vee might be the one immobile beneath me, but we both know who has the power in this situation.

The problem is nobody controls me. Ever.

I'll fulfill my role around Vee, care for her as one of us, make sure she's safe, but I refuse to yield to this power attempting to take charge of me.

I climb off Vee, and her eyes reflect my surprise. Because I moved or because our mouths touched? I step a few feet away and fold my hands beneath my arms. "I suggest you stand. I'm bored of this now."

She props herself up, hands behind on the ground, and blinks up at me. "Of course you are."

I rub my nose with the back of a hand. "Did I hurt you?"

"No." She knocks dirt from her hands and stands. "I'm fine. I told you I can look after myself." Then she winces and turns to look at her back.

"What's wrong?" I ask and step forward.

"I think I grazed my back." She holds her shirt up at the back as I bend down to examine the area. A graze the size of my palm mars her pale skin along her lower back.

"You're bleeding."

She touches the spot and screws up her face. "Not much."

I drag a hand down my cheek. "Shit, sorry, Vee. How did that happen?"

"My clothes must've bunched up behind when I landed on my back. The grounds covered in stones. It's only a graze, don't worry."

"Yeah, but still..." I step closer and pick a stray leaf from her hair. "Sorry."

"Are you *apologising* to me, Xander?"

"I meant to teach you how *not* to get hurt, not hurt you. My job's to keep you safe."

"Really, it's no big deal."

"Come inside, I'll fix you up." I incline my head to the door. "We have a first aid kit, even Horsemen hurt themselves sometimes."

Is the shocked look on her face because I'm offering to tend to her grazes or because she's still as affected by what just happened as my pounding heart is?

How much longer can I fool myself that I'm not as overwhelmed by Vee and unable to escape the effect in the way the other guys are?

11

VEE

Once inside, Xander heads to the kitchen where he reaches into an overhead cupboard and pulls out an impressive-sized box, containing enough supplies to run a small hospital ward. "Nurse in a former life?" I joke.

"If I was, I'd have better equipment."

I eye the sealed packets in the first aid kit as he rummages through. "If you're hurting, I can call Joss. He has anaesthetic properties."

"I'm fine. It's a graze, Xander. You're overreacting."

"I'm supposed to keep you safe," he says in a low voice again. "I'm not supposed to injure you."

I agree to lying on the sofa, when that's clearly not necessary either, confused by his intensity. If hurting me is a big no, then why try hand-to-hand combat? "You didn't do anything deliberately."

"My temper took over. I shouldn't lose control around you." Xander kneels on the floor holding a folded white cloth and puts a small brown bottle on the carpet. "Let me see."

I pull my shirt upwards, exposing the side of my back. He sets down the bottle and cloth, then his long fingers move along my skin. He avoids touching the cut, but sets my skin alight.

"That's a pretty nasty graze. Didn't you feel it happen?"

"I guess I was oblivious in the heat of the moment. Fight, I mean." His steady look contains the hidden Xander, and I attempt the same. *Oh, you know, because you sitting on top of and almost kissing me phased out everything but the thought of how your lips would feel.*

Xander on his knees in front of me? I laugh to myself.

"What's funny?" he asks.

"You're being friendly."

"I am friendly. When I want to be." He reaches on the floor for the small bottle, unscrews and tips the clear liquid onto a white cloth.

I've heard from the other guys how an innate desire to protect me overrides everything. I'd suspected Xander's personality interfered with that need, and I was merely a necessary link in the chain. I'd convinced myself that, to Xander, I wasn't someone to be protected, instead that he wanted me out there, doing whatever I'd been created for, straightaway.

I was wrong.

Xander moves his head closer to my body, and I jerk as he wipes the cloth over the cut.

"Omigod, Xander!" I half shriek as the skin stings.

"Jesus, Xander!" calls a voice, and the lounge door slams shut. "Seriously, you have a bedroom if you're going to be such a hypocrite."

I sit, my shirt falling back down and see a thunderous-faced Heath watching.

Xander sits back on his haunches. "Huh?"

"I... fell and grazed myself. Xander's fixing me up."

Heath's mouth opens. "Oh. I just heard you and saw him with his head..."

"I have my clothes on, Heath," I say. "You have one hell of an imagination."

"I couldn't see properly from the doorway. Guess I jumped to conclusions."

Xander laughs loudly. "If me and Vee was even a possibility, do you think we're stupid enough to do that shit where you guys can find us? Surely you and her stick to your bedroom."

I shove Xander in the shoulder. "I haven't been in Heath's bedroom. Only Joss's."

Xander's eyebrows shoot up. "With Joss in the bed?"

"Yes." *Crap.* "Not like that. Ask Ewan."

"He was there too? Both guys and you in Joss's bed?" Xander mock gasps and places a hand over his mouth. "Verity, you shock me."

I poke my tongue into my cheek and lean forward, my face almost touching his. "Why? Did you want to be there too, Xander?"

"Are you for real? You had a threesome with Joss and Ewan? Man..."

"No! Not even close," I reply.

"Yeah, if it were me I wouldn't be sharing you." He moistens his lips and looks at my mouth. "I'd be enough for you on my own."

"What's he saying, Vee?" asks Heath. "You look pissed off."

I shake my head and stand. "Can I just say something? I get that this is a weird situation between the five of us, but drop the snarky attitude, Xander."

"Honestly, not my problem if you want to share yourself, but leave me off the list. I don't share my girls."

"I'm not being *shared*," I snap. "I'm not a thing. I make my own decisions."

"So you *do* want a threesome?" asks Xander. "Or more?"

"No, I do not. But we all know this is complicated. You're the one who's annoyed with dancing around subjects. I'm being straight up about how I feel."

Xander looks over at Heath. "How do you feel about your girlfriend telling you she wants other men?"

"And there I was thinking you weren't an asshole today. Are you listening to anything I say here? I'm not his girlfriend for a start."

"Oh yeah, I hear you loud and clear." Xander stands too. "But we're not all under your spell, sweetheart."

"No?" I step closer. "Really?"

He leans in to whisper, "I'd happily take you to bed and fuck you, but that's it. Things would be out of *my* system, but you'll want more."

"Sure," I whisper back with a disbelieving snort.

"Why not try me and see?" he hisses.

His challenge elevates my heart rate as much as his fierce words. "Maybe one day I will."

A slow smile snakes across Xander's face as he steps back. "Maybe if everybody gets this sex bullshit over with, we can drop the tension and get on with our job." He turns to Heath. "Speaking of which, we need to debrief about the activities at The Warehouse last night, and I need full details about what you and Joss found on your hunt."

At the mention of last night, I drop my challenge.

"We didn't find anything, Xander. I told you," replies Heath.

"Don't care. Things to discuss. Meeting. Five minutes." He shoves the cloth and bottle at Heath. "You finish helping, Vee. I've more important shit to do than this." Xander strides to the door, passed his brother, and I blink in confusion as he heads out.

Heath rubs his face. "That escalated quickly."

"War? Escalated quickly? Are you surprised?" I'm stunned by his whiplash-inducing change in attitude to me. One minute he's concerned and helping me out, the next... this. The man cannot handle anybody disagreeing with him. Talk about attitude.

Heath crosses towards me and cups my cheek. "What happened exactly?"

"Xander was showing me some self-defence and I fell."

Heath frowns. "He should be more careful."

"I like that Xander doesn't treat me as if I'm fragile."

"Vee, how many times do I have to say this? I think we're programmed to keep you safe, somehow. Even

Xander; I bet he's feeling like shit right now. Probably why he's so pissed off."

"But I have powers; you don't need to look after me." A memory from last night flickers across my eyes, and I blink it away.

"But you don't understand or control them yet."

"*Yet.* But it's a balance. I want the opportunity to show I'm capable of being your equal and I'm not a delicate girl."

Heath smiles and cups my cheek, placing a soft kiss on my lips. "I'm still going to treat you like one, sorry."

I grit my teeth against more unwarranted fussing. Until I can prove otherwise, their attitude to me won't change. Following my experience last night, I need to get my hands on a demon and show the guys what I'm capable of. I'll figure out exactly how powerful I am; then God help anybody who tries to harm me again.

12

HEATH

Vee's insistence she gives notice she's leaving her job, rather than never returning amuses me, but she's serious. Xander doesn't comment beyond the fact I'm instructed to go with her as safety in numbers for Vee's one-week notice period.

Two days to go.

I don't see Vee at work, but her appearance at the end of each day worries me. Despite her not fitting in at the company, even after three years, Vee always smiles and exchanges polite conversation with people. Nowadays, she's distracted; the strain of the last few days caught up. She's focusing on her phone as she walks toward me now. I understand that trick, stops people talking when you want to stay quiet. I spent the last five minutes doing the same.

"Are you okay?" I ask as we leave the building. "Is this too much?"

Vee shrugs her bag onto a shoulder. "I feel weird here, like I don't belong anymore."

I resist telling her she doesn't, instead taking her hand and squeezing. "I think this will be easier once we move on. We use the house as a base and will be back, but policing the world can't be done from a small town in Oxfordshire."

She gives a weak smile. "I bet. So we're still headed north?"

"I think so. Once we clear up the mess round here." I chew my lip. She might not want to hear this. "We might need to head overseas at some point."

"Overseas?" Her eyes widen. "But I've never been further than Spain when I was a kid..." She trails off. "Or I thought so. Why?"

"The supernatural threat doesn't limit itself to a small island in Europe. Or even to the Western world, although the biggest control exists amongst the powerful countries. Once the demons take hold of the powerful countries, controlling the rest is simple."

We reach my car and Vee pauses. "Are we any closer to tracking down the demons who got away at the club the other night?"

Ewan's obsession with finding and ending the succubi gang is unusual for him. He took down one at the club, Xander two more, but not before being told there's a gang living in the area. Fury followed him home that night when the one he knew was still in the club got away. Why is Vee bothered too?

Ewan tends to get pissed off with us for wasting time

on small fry when we should be focusing on the big guys. I get that but, as Xander also argues, if we let the low-level demons out of control, they'll see the world as ripe for the picking. Ewan insists this time we make examples of them. He's probably right.

"Joss and Xander headed out today to talk to some local vampires who've indicated they've seen their sex-starved rivals around. To be honest, I think the vamps would deal with the threat themselves if we left the two sides alone."

We climb into the car and her scent from the bodywash she leaves in the bathroom reaches me, along with images of Vee in the shower. My room's next to the bathroom, and not only have I listened to the water trickle and daydreamed, I've also encountered her dressed in just a towel.

Crap. Even the thought arouses me. I shift uncomfortably.

"What's wrong?" she asks.

"Nothing." I start the car. "If they locate the gang, we're going in tonight to clear them out."

"Good. I think it would be good practice. Xander's taught me more attack moves. Ewan agrees that starting with simple enemies would be better than confronting more powerful ones." Vee stares ahead, mouth thinning. "I want to do this. I want them dead."

Whoa. I study her lined face. "They're not worth wasting more than a knife blade on. They're pathetic. Weak."

"Some of us don't have the experience you do," she snaps at me. "If I kill them I'll know I can always defend myself."

Her harsh tone doesn't sound like Vee. Maybe she's spending too much time around Xander, and he's filling her head with ideas that brute force is the way to go. "Wow, okay."

She turns a smile to me, but her eyes hold something different, adding to the stress surrounding her. "Maybe I can try both. Blind them, then stab them."

I laugh. "Perhaps you can, if your power triggers."

Vee's quiet much of the journey home until we approach the house, tyres crunching on gravel as I slow to approach the house. "Why do you still work at Alphanet?" she asks. "You could've left once you found me."

"So could you."

"I *am* leaving."

I tap my fingers on the steering wheel. "I like some normality occasionally. When we're around here, I almost feel like I have a home. In a weird way, having a job in the real world felt good. I get sick of being on the road."

Vee chews her lip as she looks at me. "Aren't you happy with being who you are?"

What do I say? That I struggle some days because I want more? That I see the real human world around me and crave to be part of it? I fight against my human side, remind myself I'm Death and don't belong. I wasn't born into a family, but thrown into a weird brotherhood with no memory of my past.

"Sometimes I want my reality to be different too," I reply. "As you may've noticed, saving the world is hard work. I like downtime."

"Working at a boring telecommunications company?"

"Spending time with a girl who's the centre of my world." I shake my head. *Shit.* "Literally. You know what I mean."

"I do." She places a hand on my leg and squeezes. "You want a girl to date. Someone ordinary. A relationship."

"Not really." *You. I want you. So bloody much*. "Just a different reality."

"Do the others know you feel like this?"

"I think we all do occasionally. Even Xander. He gets pissed off with me because sometimes I get too distracted by what he calls my sulking."

"Hah. You all spend time at pubs and clubs and hook up with girls. I think you have plenty of human in your life."

"Yeah, but that's not the same, Vee."

My words close down the conversation, and when I glance at her, there's a sadness in her downturned mouth. I mentally kick myself. By sharing my struggles, have I reminded her of what she thought was true and what she lost?

13

Vee

Heath parks his car on a suburban street as we did when we visited Portia, but this time the fancy houses and perfect gardens are missing. This street is at the back of a sprawling council estate, where broken cars sit on the road rather than upmarket models on driveways.

Nowadays, the residents are a mix of the original council residents and those who've bought the houses. Most are rentals, including the one we're eyeing up now with overgrown front lawn and dirty windows.

"Don't you think all five of us is a bit of overkill for a few pathetic demons?" asks Joss. "They're not exactly powerful."

"This will take us a few minutes, and then we can

head out for a celebratory pint, don't worry," Heath puts in.

Despite my shaking nerves and anger I'm about to slaughter those responsible for my assault the other night, his words amuse me. "A quick kill on the way to the pub? You guys never cease to amuse me."

"Why waste an evening?" says Joss with a grin and opens the door. "Are they definitely home, Ewan? Need me to check?"

"Yeah. Xander tracked them before."

I'm sandwiched between Ewan and Heath in the back, something I'm not unhappy about and led to my mind drifting in directions that would've shocked me in the past. I don't have any intention of asking them, but there's something arousing at the thought of both guys um... "tending to my sexual needs" as much as they tend to all my others, if I let them.

Focus. Do not picture them naked.

"Two take the front of the house, two the rear," says Xander as he climbs out.

"Um? What about your Fifth?" I ask.

"With me," says Ewan before Xander can reply. "The rear."

I follow Ewan and Joss around to the end of the street, so we can head down the lane and to the back of the houses. We pass a row of graffitied garages and paved areas, some with cars parked on them and others with washing hung on lines.

"This one," says Joss in a low voice.

A flaking wooden gate leads into the unevenly paved yard, weeds pushing through the gaps. A light shines in an upstairs room behind a thin curtain, but the room in front of us, to the left of the back door, is dark. Ewan heads to the door and examines it.

"Dead bolt. We either kick the door down or wait for a demon to run out when the guys break in the front." A knife flashes as he takes it from his pocket. "I'm all for getting straight into this."

"Boring!" exclaims Joss. "Prime the door."

"Prime?" I ask.

"Yeah. True." Ewan glances at my confusion. "I can add something nice and painful. The amount of bacteria for me to use around here's plentiful."

Joss straightens as noise begins in the house. A male yell, footsteps running upstairs. "Not sure you'll have time."

The door flings open and a girl, wild-eyed and holding a white shirt against her naked torso, stands on the doorstep. Ewan steps forward and Joss grabs his arm. "No. She's human. Victim probably."

The girl spots our knife and turns back to the house with a scream, but Joss rushes passed and steps in the way. "It's okay. We're not here to hurt you."

"Those men... they're attacking my friends!" She looks at me, then back to Joss. "Is this about drugs? I can tell you where the drugs are. Please don't hurt me."

I step forward and address her in a gentle voice. "It's cold out here. Maybe put your shirt on?"

She frowns down at the shirt in her hand. "Right. I didn't realise. When did I take that off?"

The anger I'm containing seethes as I spot her unbuttoned jeans too. I could've been her. "Do you know these people?"

"Yes. Kind of. We met them last week. Do they owe

you money? They're not bad people, they don't deserve to die!"

Her voice rises into a shriek and Ewan swears under his breath. "Get the girl back inside!"

"No!" she half screams. "Don't touch me!"

"Joss!" Ewan jabs a finger at the girl. "Calm her down."

"It's okay," I say in a low voice as she flinches away from Joss's attempted touch. "We're not going to hurt you. We're here to help."

"Yeah, police, undercover," says Ewan and half drags her inside.

I groan. "Seriously?" I mouth at Joss.

"Don't you dare tell her the truth," he says and nudges me with his elbow, grinning.

How can he grin right now?

The door leads into a filthy kitchen, where ashtrays filled with cigarette butts and empty cans and bottles vie for space on the Formica table and kitchen counter. I wrinkle my nose at the mixed scent—mould, rotting food, and unmistakable sickly drug smell.

"Sit with her," says Joss and pulls out a metal chair from under the table.

"No," I say. "I came here to"—I glance at the girl—"Deal with the problem."

"I think—" he begins.

"You sit with her," interrupts Ewan. "Vee, come with me."

"What?" Joss frowns. "Why?"

He doesn't get a response as Ewan drags me through the next doorway and into a smoke-filled lounge room. Xander stands in the corner, over a girl's lifeless body as Heath chases another who's running upstairs.

The sight shocks me, but I need to tell myself these aren't people. The guys aren't killing women but demons. A young guy on the sofa, black hair, piercings, blinks at us through a drugged haze as he buttons his jeans. "What the fuck?"

His voice is weak as he struggles to stand. This isn't only drugs; the succubus on the floor must be responsible for his state because the guy's shirt's open and eyes glazed, face pale.

"Fun's over. Thank us for saving your life," growls Xander. He jabs a finger toward the stairs. "Ewan. Some ran upstairs. We think there're more in the bedrooms. Heath's up there."

I shove Ewan to one side and charge up the stairs. My shoes stick to a stained carpet, and I hear a woman scream behind a door to my right. My blood chills. I bloody hope that's Heath and a demon. Light filters beneath another door in front of me. Ewan kicks at the door to my left, face impassive.

Adrenaline pushes me forward, and I throw open the third door.

A girl with long red hair lies on the bed. Naked. Unconscious. I want to look away but the horror drives reality home. A man steps away from her, backing up as he hastily puts jeans on and looks at me.

Not a man. A demon. The other guy from the club.

Stocky. Vibrant green hair, but this time with a drunk look on his face from feeding on the girl. This is the first demon who touched me that night, by the bathrooms and was involved in my assault. My stomach turns as I look between him and the bed, imagining my face as the girl's. Shit. Is she unconscious or dead?

Fury grips me and builds with a sudden intensity. *Fucking demon bastard.*

My control snaps, and I lunge at the guy with my knife; he sidesteps me. "Back for more?" he sneers. "I heard my friend was rudely interrupted when you were having fun the other night."

His arrogance surpasses any fear this incubus has for me as he steps forward and attempts to close his hand around mine holding the knife.

"You don't fucking touch me!" I shout and hold the point towards his face. "You really don't know who you're messing with."

He laughs. "Of course I do. We knew. You think you're special? Untouchable? The perfect Fifth? You don't have the guts to do anything; the weak female who can't do anything without the Four around."

"Wrong!" I snarl and rush him, slamming a hand into his chest. My strength surprises us both as his back hits the wall, head smacking against the plaster. The demon blinks, dazed for a moment, and the overwhelming desire to kill him frightens me.

"Go on," he hisses. "I'm too human looking. You're scared."

The naked girl. His mocking. The memories. A pressure begins behind my skull, one I recognise from Portia's house. Only this time I'm alone; no Xander. This strength is all me—and I'm going to bloody use it.

"I'm not scared of you. Or anybody," I snarl.

His eyes widen as my skin takes on a luminescence, white light building as my blood becomes lava-hot and courses through my veins.

His struggling stops, frozen in place, as the light fills

the room. This time I keep my eyes open and watch as the light focuses into a snaking beam that coils around the incubus, tightening across his body before it explodes with a force that fills the room and knocks me back from him.

This isn't the same as last time. This is me and only me. I watch with triumph as the guy's eyes blacken, his form shifting from that of a younger guy into the twisted visage of a demon. His unnaturally pointed features and a cruel turn to his wide mouth with runes cover his red skin reveals his true form.

"I don't think you look very human," I hiss and bury the knife into his chest, to the place Xander repeatedly showed me in practice over the last few days. The sneer doesn't leave his face as he sinks to the carpet. My hand shakes as I pull at the knife protruding from his chest.

His closed eyes snap open. "Try harder," he rasps. The demon places a hand on the wall, and I'm momentarily arrested as he pulls himself to his feet, blood spreading into a stain across his chest.

How was that not enough? I thought they were weak?

The heat in my veins changes, tingle switching to a pain resembling electric shocks spreading down my arm and into my fingertips. I drop the knife in surprise as the light surrounding my hand crackles into energy.

The need to end his life overwhelms me again, a strange instinct taking over my fear, and I hold my palms out, approaching him. A visible white lightning-like power shoots from my hands towards his chest, and he jerks before dropping to the floor; a dead weight.

This time, as I stare down, head and hands hurting, he doesn't move. I poke him with my boot. Dead.

The girl.

I grab a blanket scrunched on the bed corner and cover her body before anybody else appears. She's violated enough without anybody else seeing her naked. Despite the heavy make-up, her face is soft, innocent. Tears push their way into my eyes. Will she remember what happened to her? I bend down and touch the girl's neck, praying for a pulse. Weak.

"Was it him?" I look up to a more dishevelled than usual Ewan. "Is he the demon from the club I couldn't find?"

I nod. "Were there more?"

"Yeah. Six. In pairs. Mostly attacking and oblivious when we arrived." His face contorts back to anger as he notices the girl on the bed. "I bloody hope she isn't dead."

"No. Weak."

"Fucking bastards!" He crosses his arms and eyes the girl. "I don't want to touch and scare her. Will you sit here until she wakes up?"

Ewan's too fired up to notice, but I'm ready to reach out, to ask him to tell me everything's okay. Whatever gripped my body frightens me, and I stare at my still tingling fingers. The truth hits me like a wall of water.

I took on the unrelenting fury of War, and I conjured Death. I blinded with Truth and revealed the demon's deceptive appearance. Do I possess Joss's and Ewan's powers too?

I tuck shaking hands beneath my arms and nod. Ewan makes to leave the room and pauses. He stares at the dead incubus for a few moments, lips thinning as his brow pulls deep, before he turns his eyes to mine. "Wish

I'd had the pleasure of killing the bastard, but great job, Vee."

I sink onto the bed as he strides back out the door. *Great job?* Bloody hell. Is this a mundane task to perform before an evening out, the way I joked?

The girl on the bed stirs, blinking up at me in a sleepy haze before her face transforms into panicked horror to match her friend who tried to run outside. She opens her mouth, ready to scream, and I place a hand on her shoulder. The girl's mouth closes again as she grasps my fingers before she drops forward against me, head against my chest. The girl's back moves as she sobs, and unsure what to do, I stroke her hair and will the fear to leave.

Gradually, she stills and relaxes, and I close my eyes, fortified by a new energy replacing the exhaustion from fighting the demon. I snap them open again.

I have Joss's power too.

14

Vee

Another guy and a girl were in the upstairs rooms Xander and Ewan went into. Add in the guy from the sofa and girl on the bed, plus the one who tried to run, and we have five witnesses to the demons' deaths, or aftermath. The guys are drugged, and the girls are high too. Caused by magic or the white powder on the table? All are freaked out, understandably, since they just witnessed multiple murders, and I watch the Four, curious how they deal with this situation.

Judging by their handling, this isn't an uncommon state of affairs for them. Xander gathers the group into the lounge room and frightens the group into silence, of course. He informs them we're undercover detectives on a drug sting and threatens to arrest them for possession, waving around a bag containing enough white powder to land them a hefty prison sentence. He impresses on them that the gang were dangerous and would've killed everybody. I'm as caught up in his whirlwind explanation as they are; his authority's clear.

Finally, he warns them police backup is on the way and that if they don't leave, they'll be taken in for questioning. Sofa guy doesn't need telling twice and stumbles out of the house in seconds.

"I bet he already has a criminal record," mutters Heath.

Joss is gentler. He sits beside the girls and they look back at him, their swimming eyes focusing on his face. I don't hear his words to them, but they relax and nod, tears drying as they sink back on the seats.

I turn away and walk into the kitchen, towards the open back door where I sit on the step and stare across the yard towards the garages opposite. Too many lies around me. If I open my big mouth, things could become complicated.

Heath perches beside me and squeezes my leg. "You okay?"

"Think so. Not really. I don't know." My voice catches.

"Vee..." He wraps an arm around my shoulder and pulls me close. "What happened?"

How do I explain this? "I think I'm War and Death too."

"Huh?" He pulls away. "What do you mean?"

I hold out my hands, convinced I'll find evidence, but there's none but a faint glow. "When I fought the incubus, I was strong, stronger than usual. And angrier. My light turned into something else. I don't know... something like electricity came from my fingers. Hit the demon in the chest and killed him, the way I saw you at Portia's. That's your power, isn't it? And the strength is Xander's?"

"Holy crap," he says in a low voice. "But I wasn't there."

"I don't think you need to be," I whisper. "This gets weirder. The girl... I calmed her down when she was ready to scream the house down. Like Joss does." Heath touches my face, and I curl my fingers around his. "Do you think I am? Am I made up of all of you?"

Heath kisses my forehead. "No, you're Verity, and you're Truth. But I think we just discovered what powers you have."

I swallow. "All of them?"

"Looks that way. Remind me never to piss you off." I crack a smile at his attempt to lighten my situation. "This is a game changer, Vee. How do you feel about it?"

"Not sure. Not scared, more confused." I rest my head against his shoulder, and focus on my breathing, on his scent. His comfort doesn't match Joss's, but I've kissed and touched this man; felt his care for me before. "Relieved that I can match you. I think you guys will need to believe I can look after myself now."

"I'm bloody sure you can. Did you choose to use the powers when you were upstairs?"

"Not sure. I was angry when I saw the girl on the bed. I think that triggered War's power against the incubus. Then my own, but instead of amplifying one of you it revealed the Truth. He didn't die which triggered the need to use the Death inside me. And then after... I starved the girl of her fear. Famine."

"And Pestilence?"

I chew on the inside of my mouth. "No. Not this time, anyway."

"Weird. Well, maybe the more you use the powers, the easier they'll come."

I laugh softly. "You make it sound as if I'm learning a new sport."

"It kind of is."

"You see killing as sport?"

Heath shrugs. "No. Well, sometimes. Thrill of the chase and all that."

Somebody touches my hair, and I tip my head backwards to look at Joss. "How are you feeling, Vee?"

"Overwhelmed."

"Understandable." He sits the otherside of me and places a hand on my leg. "Ready for a drink?"

"A drink?"

"The pub? These guys promised me a beer."

How can they switch off from this as easily? They just freaking chased and killed demons, dealt with horrified victims, and all they can think about is a trip to the pub?

I shift out of Heath's embrace. "No, thanks. I'd rather go home. In fact, I'd like to get out of here before the police arrive."

"We are the police, remember?" says Joss.

"The real police," I say in a low voice. "Somebody must've called them."

"Maybe, maybe not. People don't like to interfere," Heath says.

"When women are screaming?" Heath and Joss exchange a look, and although I understand people's "don't interfere" attitude, morally that's wrong. The human race is disappointing.

No, surely somebody must've called the police.

"I'll take her. You guys help Xander clear up." Again, I

hear those words *clear up*, this time spoken by Ewan. He walks over and sits on a nearby kitchen chair, resting elbows on his knees and hands beneath his chin.

"You just want an excuse to be alone with Vee again," says Joss. "Impress her with a ride." He pauses and sniggers. "On your bike."

Ewan scowls, and I sigh and shift away from Heath and Joss. "Tomorrow, I want to talk to you all about something."

"Sounds interesting," says Joss.

"Just a few concerns. Some ground rules."

"Ooh, Vee has rules for us now she's powerful. Can't wait to see what Xan-the-man has to say about that." Joss rubs his hands together. "Love it!"

"I can take you home if you want?" asks Heath.

"No dude, you have the SUV and are designated driver. We won't all fit on Ewan's bike if he's the one who stays!"

I suppress a laugh. "He's right. Is that okay with you?" I ask Ewan. "I'll go to the pub if you really want to as well."

"No, Vee." He's firm, the gruff Ewan; the only one I experience since the night at the club. "You want to go, I'll take you."

"You'll take care of her, yeah?" asks Joss and looks between us, then wags a finger at Ewan. "But not too well."

"Nah, they'll probably geek out with their laptops," says Heath.

I attempt a smile but I'm still shaking like jelly after the last half an hour. The evening's events catch up with the old, human Vee, as she attempts to reconcile this new one.

Heath stands. "I half wish you hadn't come with us tonight."

"I told you, I had to. I feel better now I've killed him—demons. I feel like I can do what I'm created for."

The following silence fills with low voices from the other room and nobody looks at me. *Created*. Well, I was, but how?

"You're still a human girl, Vee."

"No. I'm the Fifth," I say through gritted teeth. "And I'm your equal."

"I don't think you are." I spin around where Xander stands in the doorway between the kitchen and the lounge, arms holding onto the top of the frame. His T-shirt rides up, revealing rock hard abs I'm unfortunately drawn to stare at. He's lost some of the anger that blackened his face into something frightening, but stress surrounds him still.

My ebbing anger flows again, as I ready a stream of unpleasant words to throw at him.

A muscle twitches in his cheek, the amusement grating further. "I mean, I think you're superior to us, Vee."

"Oh." The word rushes out with a surprised breath, but of course, he has to back his words up with something negative.

"But right now, you're new to us. We need to figure all this out. Tonight was step one. Until then, *you* have to accept we're going to treat you differently to the way we treat each other." He pauses. "You're too human still."

A stand-off ensues as I hold his look, refusing to back down into the weakness he seems to think underpins me. I stride towards him so my next words aren't audible to the others. He drops his hands from the frame as I approach.

"It's not my fault you're intimidated by me," I whisper. His features remain unmoved. "Or threatened? Is that it?"

Xander's focus stays on my face, and I'm aware in the silence the other guys must watch us. He runs his tongue along his bottom lip. "Neither."

I don't say the next word, but my raised brow replies: you're a liar. "Wait until I give you all the details about what happened to me tonight. Then you might change your tune."

I turn back to the curious looks from Heath, Joss, and Ewan.

"Can we leave now, Ewan?"

15

Vee

My first time on a motorcycle terrifies me. Ridiculous, considering everything that's happened to me in the last few days, but I am. I dressed in jeans and a dark jacket tonight, nothing too bulky for my extracurricular activities. Apparently this isn't warm enough for a bike ride, as Ewan removes his leather jacket and insists I wear it. I spend the journey engulfed by his coat, clinging to him with my face buried in his back. Or as buried as I can manage considering I'm wearing his heavy helmet. At least this gives me an extra barrier between the world storming passed my head.

I'd ask Ewan to slow down, but he'd never hear me.

My arms barely fit around his broad frame, his powerful back muscles tensed as he speeds along country lanes. My—his—jacket is unzipped and his T-shirt presses against me, his body beneath warming mine, and I wish I could place my cheek against him.

At the house, I attempt to climb from the bike like a seasoned professional, but Ewan needs to help me stand on shaky legs, then assist with the helmet I struggle to unstrap with my cold fingers. My hair's damp with perspiration, and I suck in the fresh night air.

"Wow, you look like you really enjoyed that," he says sarcastically.

I stand with his jacket sleeves hanging over my hands, like a little kid trying on adult clothes. "My first time."

"Serious? Why didn't you say, and I could've been gentler?" He bites his lip. "I would've slowed down a bit until you were comfortable."

Was that a hint of innuendo? Unable to ready a comeback, I stride towards the farmhouse. The house holds a hominess I never expected, and it's a relief to be in a sanctuary away from the monsters in the night. Heath's joke about "geeking out" echoes, and the temptation to pull out my laptop and switch the world off grows as I follow Ewan into the cool kitchen. I shrug off his jacket and place it over a chair.

"I need some Horseman fuel," says Ewan and grins as he opens the fridge and takes two bottles. "Joss bought you some cider."

I stare at the second bottle in his hand. "I was kidding about that. I'm not really into drinking."

"Yeah, I noticed that when we went to the W—" He cuts himself dead as I turn my look to the floor. "Yeah. Anyway."

"Maybe I'll have that cider." I take the bottle.

We stand awkwardly, yet again, and I pick at the label on my bottle. "So, did you hear the news?"

"What news?"

"Apparently I have everybody's power." I swig as Ewan stares at me. "I only had a chance to tell Heath before we left."

"Holy crap." Ewan grips his bottle. "How do you know?"

I explain to Ewan, the same way I told Heath, attempting not to show how scared I am by everything. But instead of sharing Heath's stunned reaction, Ewan nods.

"I thought so," he says as I finish. "Makes sense to me why we're so glued to you. If you have a piece of each Horseman's power, you have a piece of us. We need to protect you the way we would ourselves."

"But I thought I just amplified your powers."

"So did we, especially after what happened with you and Xander at Portia's. This is a bloody big shock, and I can't wait to see Xander's face when he finds out he was wrong."

"If it means Xander has extra ammunition at his disposal, I'm sure he'll be fine."

Ewan shakes his head. "Your humour never fools me, Vee. I don't need to be Joss to see how worried you are by this. Since we came into the house, you haven't stopped fidgeting, and you're tenser than I've seen before." He points at me. "If you grip that bottle any harder, you're going to break it."

I pull out a chair and sit. Ewan stands, arms crossed, lips pursed. "What?" I ask.

"I wonder why you didn't demonstrate my power?"

"Maybe I didn't need to tonight?" I suggest.

"Or maybe you feel closer to the other guys." He looks passed me and drinks slowly. "Because we're kind of distant, aren't we? Even you and Xander, however much you clash, there's a closeness. Heath, he's the guy you first met, and I think that makes a difference. Joss helps you a lot. You're close to him. Me? I'm a reminder of what happened to you the other night. I can't help you in the way Joss could right now."

"That's not true, and I don't need Joss to make me feel better."

Ewan rubs his mouth as he studies me. "But you're different towards me after the night at the club, Vee."

Our eyes meet for more than a few seconds for the first time in days. "So are you."

"I didn't tell the guys about the incubus attack, like you asked."

"I know. Thank you."

Ewan runs a hand across the top of his head, hair messing further, and his capped sleeve slides to reveal more tattoos. "I feel like you blame me somehow."

"I don't blame you," I say in a low voice. "It's just... things are odd."

"Because the incubus looked like me?" he blurts.

I'm caught in his steady gaze, in the concern behind his green eyes. Initially, I took Heath to be the sensitive guy with his care and attention, how he spoke his mind with a need for me to understand him. As the days pass, Ewan's nature becomes plainer. He's moody, yes, not as sensitive to people around him as Joss, but his quiet nature holds deeper thinking. I remember the first day, when he insisted on telling me as much as he could—or was allowed.

"There's a lot we never spoke about, isn't there?" I ask him.

He pulls out a chair and sits beside me. "Things fucked up between us."

"Did they?"

"Yeah. I was the one who told you about... your lack of a past." I smile at his term. "Then I'm a reminder of the night a demon assaulted you. Both times I failed to protect you."

I reach out and curl my fingers around his. "Tonight I looked after myself. I'm fine."

His face is lined with worry as he looks back. "You need to accept you're our number one priority, which is why I'm struggling here. I feel I have to apologise for something I didn't do." His heavy brow deepens. "I would never have touched you and kissed you like that."

I swallow down my disappointment and pull my hand away. "Never?"

"I told you the first day we spoke why I couldn't."

I slide my hand down Ewan's arm and lace my fingers through his again. He looks down in surprise and rubs his thumb across the back of my hand, the pad rough against my soft skin.

"You have this all wrong," I whisper and look down at where our hands connect. "There's a different reason why I'm finding it hard to be around you. I know the demon wasn't you but..." I trail off.

I need to say the words, to admit the truth lighting up every time I look at Ewan and the exact reason why.

"I wanted the person who kissed me to be you, Ewan.

THE FOUR HORSEMEN: BOUND

I saw the way you looked at me when we left the house for the club, and nobody ever looked at me like that before."

He gives a rare smile, one that spreads to his eyes. "Nobody ever stared at your drop-dead-gorgeous body? Yeah, right. I thought you couldn't lie?"

"No. But the way you did was different. It wasn't just 'appreciating the view.' You looked me in the eyes too, and there was something different, like a respect."

"Or a reverence?" he says with a laugh. "You're amazing and I crave you. To be around you. Horseman thing," he corrects.

My chest flutters at his words, at how his fingers grip mine tighter.

"And now... everything's confused. When the memories seep in, they're your hands and mouth on me; you're the one making me feel as if I can switch off from this, escape somewhere else, even if it's just for a short time." I stare at his mouth. "You're the one I wanted that night. Want now."

Ewan's dark-eyed look winds around my heart. "You make your own decisions, remember?"

I reach out and touch Ewan. His stubble's longer than Heath's is making his face rougher against my fingers. Hair dips into his eyes and half-curled strands touch his ears. I attempt to quash the effect he has on me, to deny this is human as well as supernatural, but there's no letting go of the physical attraction.

In a moment ruled by my body and not my brain, where I fool myself this is merely a supernatural connection, I move my face towards his.

"I do," I whisper.

Ewan's large hand grips the back of my head, fingers digging into my hair and he rests his head on mine. "Think about this, Vee."

"I am," I mumble and move my lips closer.

He closes his eyes the moment my breath mingles with his, unable to escape the effect.

"I need you to replace the false you with the real one." His uptick in breathing tells me what I need to know. He understands exactly what I mean. "Ewan, I've spent days imagining what this would really be like with you."

I tense as his grip on my hair tightens, forehead firmly against mine. "Why?"

"Because I think you want me, too. And I want to do this. With you."

I climb onto Ewan's lap and his dark eyes edge between surprise and lust. My legs rest either side of his hips, and he holds my ass hard against him. I expected a rough kiss, but when our mouths meet his lips move gently against mine before he teases his tongue into my mouth. I grasp his head hard as he digs his fingers into my thighs, and deepens the kiss.

The streaming memories and emotions between us match those I felt with Heath; the experience amplified beyond the physical I felt from the fake Ewan's kiss. His touch and taste pull everything tight inside, arousal as instant as if he's flicked a switch. I want comfort, but different to that Joss gives. I'm loved by these men, and right now, I need to let go of my control around them and take our physical connection to the next step.

Am I high on my new powers? Liberated by the fact I'm stronger than them all? I don't care because this feels right.

We remain, bodies interlocking and mouths unwilling to part as we release the frustration we have with each other in tugging lips, nipping skin, and long, hard kisses. I tip my head back as he lands kisses along my neck, hands sliding beneath my shirt and along my side.

"We're alone for how long," I whisper, fingers lost in his hair.

"They'll contact me first." He nods at the phone, but he's disoriented by desire the same as I am. "We're fine."

I hold his broad shoulders, and he circles my weight in his arms. "Are we?"

The unspoken passes but I say the words anyway, the one that changes our dynamic forever. "Yes. We are."

Still he hesitates, a characteristic I never expected from the guy with his powerful bulk and edgy look. I yank his T-shirt upwards; Ewan grabs the collar and pulls it over his shoulders with one hand. I watch the movement, at muscles moving under his skin, and the honed magnificence I stared at in the kitchen days ago revealed again.

Holy hotness. This is why I fantasise about this man.

Ewan's kiss and touch unleashes, and I'm suffocated by the passion pouring from his body into mine. We struggle with clothes, mine following his T-shirt onto the floor, until I'm naked apart from my underwear as thin barriers between us.

I straddle Ewan again, and his erection pushes against his jeans, between us; I unashamedly rub myself against him. His rough denim scrapes my skin in the same way his scruff does, shooting heat and a welcome ache through me.

We pause, and I wrap his face between my small hands, holding onto the moment. My body aches, the heavy feeling between my legs growing. Ewan cups my breast, and I shiver as his large thumb pushes across the peaked nipple. He closes his mouth over, teasing with his tongue. His gentleness doesn't match the forceful need growing inside me.

"Ewan?" He doesn't respond. "Stop holding back."

"Don't say that," he growls, and runs his tongue across my skin.

"You hold back too much, Ewan. Not just with me, but—"

"Shut up." His mouth crashes onto mine, his touch exploding fireworks beneath my skin. He grips my hair and pulls my head back, and I can barely breathe, unable to move as he deepens the kiss. I'm lost to this moment and to him as I spin away from the world. Lips still on mine, he stands, one arm around my waist, my legs around his, and pushes everything on the kitchen table aside.

A glass spins to the floor and shatters.

He lays me down, and I wriggle against the table's cold beneath my back.

I murmur something, and I don't know what; my mind can't focus on anything but the aching need for Ewan. He growls my name and pushes my panties to one side, his fingers seeking my clit, his breath harder against my face, as he glides the tips along my wetness. I move myself against his hand, and Ewan's finger pushes inside me. The sensation jolts through my body, and I catch my breath as Ewan strokes a spot inside hardwired to the rest of my body.

I dig my fingers into Ewan's back, running my hands across his powerful shoulders, as he gives himself over to pleasuring me. The pressure and I spiral to the edge, blood pulsing in my ears, the need for release shaking through my body. I'm aware the moans in the room are coming from my mouth; but I no longer care as my vision blurs, close to the edge.

I grab Ewan's hair and breathe out at him to stop, and he looks up at me, eyes shining, before running his tongue along his lips.

"I want more than this," I croak out.

He moves back towards me, kissing along my heated skin, before covering my body beneath his weight and strength. "I don't think that's a good idea."

No. *No*. My raging hormones take over again, and my fingers go to his jean's buttons. "Why?" Ewan squeezes his eyes shut, lips parting as I push my hand inside his jeans and curl my fingers around his hard length.

"Because we need things to stay calm, and this isn't calm." His hoarse voice disagrees with his words. "Vee. Stop."

I run my hand along him. Maybe if I'd had sex within the last few months, I wouldn't be as driven to get as up close and personal with one of the guys as this, but a girl deserves some fun, right?

We return to fierce kissing, almost bumping teeth, pouring our denied needs into each other. He slides his fingers along my slick heat again with one hand, and uncurls my fingers from him with the other. Hair sticks to his forehead as he looks back down at me.

"You have no idea the amount of self-control it's taking not to pull these off and keep going." He hooks a thumb through the side of my panties. "But I'm going to prove to myself I have some around you."

I groan with frustration. "You don't need to prove anything."

Again, he closes his eyes and takes a sharp breath. Ewan slides his mouth across my breasts and down to my belly, inch by tormenting inch, and my body buzzes in anticipation.

"Fuck it," he mutters and pulls at my panties, down my legs, and they drop to the floor.

He switches to kissing along my thigh, and his hot breath caresses my heated flesh, before he swipes his tongue along my wet centre. His mouth covers me as he leisurely draws his tongue the length of me until he reaches my clit, teasing. Lightning arcs from the place his tongue touches, through my limbs, and I close my eyes, yielding.

I grip his hair again as he thrusts two fingers back inside me. His tongue skillfully strokes and teases, as he sucks on my clit until I'm heading upwards again. This man can do things with his tongue I never imagined possible, each stroke pushing me further into a natural high, driving me out of my mind, and craving one thing. More. Him. Everything.

Ewan pulls me to the blinding edge, burying his face further between my legs. His day's growth scratches, the harsh contrast to the soft adding to my arousal. The rhythm of his tongue and fingers against the soft spot inside, drag me into an intensity I've never experienced. Blood roars through my ears, my vision blackens. The orgasm shatters me, body and soul.

I'm dragged down from where I float around with the

stars in my eyes as Ewan kisses along my belly, and I wrap my shaking legs around him. Now he will, surely. He's a guy and has his needs too. His lips touch mine, briefly, and then he looks down, chest rising and falling rapidly. I reach out for him again, aching to feel him moving inside me.

"I'm not about do anything else, Vee," he says, voice hoarse.

"What?"

"I can't do this with you right now."

"On the table? We can move?"

He chuckles at me as I begin to slide off. "No. I think we need to wait until things are less charged between the five of us before taking that step."

"What?" I repeat. "Don't you want to?"

His broad palm covers my cheek. "Hell, yes. More than anything but not like this."

"I'm good with it, seriously."

"Vee, I have a lot I want to do to you, but we could be interrupted at any minute. Not what I want." He sits back and pulls me upwards, arms surrounding my waist. He rests his head against my breasts, my heart thumping against his cheek.

As if fate conspires against my decision to go all out to persuade Ewan he's wrong, his phone buzzes.

Dark eyes on me still, he takes the phone and answers. "Yeah." Ewan clears his throat. "Yeah?"

There should be something awkward about sitting naked on a man whose not strictly your lover as the real world shoves its way in.

"How long?" he asks, eyes on his hand resting on my hip. He traces a circle and I shiver. "Cool." Another pause as he listens with a furrowed brow. "Yeah? Good. See you in half an hour."

I chew the edge of my lip as Ewan's interest returns to me, fingers softer against my skin after his bruising touch. He places his lips on my forehead, a soothing spot between my eyes.

"Half an hour? That's time," I ask ever hopeful.

"Half an hour to clear your clothes off the floor," he whispers.

I smack him in the chest. "You pick them up, since you put them there."

He moves away and looks down, and I fight pouting as he buttons his jeans. "Uh huh. Then you'll need to explain to the others why I'm naked on the dining table."

Ewan smiles, the strain often surrounding him lost from his face, the way it was in the moments between us. He strokes my cheek, studying my face in a way that flips my stomach. Not just the desire he's holding back, but as if I'm the centre of his world. "I don't have Joss's skills, but I'd like to hold you for tonight."

I play my fingers along his lips. "I guess it's about time I tried someone else's bed. I might have more fun than in Joss's."

He arches a brow. "I said, hold you."

I exaggerate a frown and pout. "Fine. Maybe next time?"

Ewan picks up my clothes and drops them in my lap. "Next time. The chances I'll exercise anything close to that control again are slim to none."

I bite my lip. "I'm happy you said 'next time'."

16

EWAN

My first thought when I wake? Shit, what did I do? Not because I regret what happened, but because I'm hers now. Here I am the guy who told her we needed to avoid this situation, and I'm the first she shares herself with. Vee invites me to touch that awesome body, pour our frustration into pleasure, and blow both our minds. Like I'm gonna say no. As if any one of us would, including the constantly in denial Xander.

I grab my jeans from my bedroom floor and pull them on, gazing at the empty bed, sheet still creased with Vee's shape. How the fuck did I sleep with her naked body in my arms and not unleash what she asked from me? Man, I deserve a fucking medal. But I'm trying to respect her—

and the others. It's early days, and we need less conflict not more.

But we've spoken when Vee isn't around, acknowledging she's more than just some chick who's joined our group. Even Heath agrees none of us could claim her as theirs, and that she told him and Xander as much.

Now we've discovered her real power, that she already holds a part of each Horseman, this makes more sense. Where do we go from here as a group? I guess we'll find out soon.

I believed that the moment Vee walked into our lives everything changed, but now I understand. The chaos her arrival caused doesn't come close to what she's capable of doing to us all.

Vee's in the kitchen when I walk downstairs. A black and grey shirt from my bedroom floor covers her body, stopping just beneath her ass, stirring more than just the memories inside me. She leans against the kitchen counter, chipped blue mug in hand.

"I think you guys need a proper coffee machine. I can't stand drinking this instant stuff." Vee pulls a face. I blink at her; she focuses on weird shit sometimes. "I understand—you don't have time for frivolity when you're saving the world, but decent coffee? Everybody needs decent coffee."

Vee smiles into the mug, amused by her own joke. "I'll get Joss onto it," I reply.

She steps towards me and places her soft hand on my cheek, lips briefly touching mine. I wrap an arm around her waist and she trips, almost spilling her drink.

"How are you feeling?" I ask.

"Better now I've dealt with a couple of things over the last twenty-four hours."

"Like me, you mean?" I arch a brow.

She slaps my bare chest. "And the demon. I feel more able to be this... whatever I am."

"I think you're amazing," I kiss her forehead. "In a lot of ways."

"But you think last night was wrong?" she asks. "You're hesitant."

"I'm worried about the other guys."

Her expression surprises me. I'd expected some doubt, maybe even her avoiding me this morning, but she's genuinely confused. "This whole situation is different to usual."

"That's one word to describe it." I let her go and search for my own mug. When I turn back around, Vee's watching as she drinks, eyes dark the way they were last night as she rakes her gaze over my naked chest. "Need me to put my shirt on so you can control yourself?" I ask her.

"You want me to take your shirt off? Okay." Vee's fingers go to the buttons and I freeze, convinced she'll get naked in the kitchen for a second time, but she laughs again.

I'm three steps away from heading over to kiss her, absorb some of her happiness the way Joss can from people, because with her that's something I haven't felt for a long time. But Xander walks into the kitchen from outside, red cheeked from his usual morning walk. He flicks a look between us, then spends a good few seconds studying the point my shirt stops and Vee's smooth tanned legs start. The partially unbuttoned shirt also attracts his attention. *Yeah, she's naked under there, Xander.*

I'm unsurprised by the way they look at each other—his attempt at impassiveness marred by the effect she has that he denies. I've spotted something I don't think Xander has; she's up to his challenge, and he has no hope of winning.

"Aren't you cold, Vee?" he asks. "You're not wearing much."

"A little, but I needed a drink."

He unzips his jacket and gestures at Vee. "Nice shirt, hey, Ewan? Yours, isn't it?"

We glance at each other, and Xander's mouth tugs into a knowing smile. "Ha, Ewan! Now I didn't expect *this*."

What do I say? Vee's nonplussed; she drains her mug and sets it in the sink.

"I heard Joss slept in his own bed last night," Xander continues. "Alone. Where were you, Vee?"

I blow air into my cheeks. "I expect Joss and Heath'll be up soon. Maybe get dressed, Vee?"

"That was next on my list." She smiles at me, and *hell* I want her to kiss me.

Xander crosses his arms and watches Vee's ass as she leaves the room. He turns to me. "Dude, you are in so much trouble."

17

Vee

I spend longer than usual in the shower as I think about the last night's events. I can definitively say I have never had a night like that before. Discovering I had one power had been a shock, and discovering I have several more halfway terrifies me. What if I can't control them? How *do* I control them?

And then there was Ewan.

Omigod, last night there was Ewan. And kissing. And touching. And *hell*, so much more than I imagined would happen. I close my eyes and soak up the arousing memories as my hair soaks the water flowing onto me. Why don't I feel weird about what happened? Yes, I wanted him, but I want Heath too. And Joss. Xander? No. But I'm in denial because I've imagined us battling out our conflict into a different, more naked direction.

Is this wrong? I've struggled with the idea since I arrived. I shouldn't want all the guys but I do, and I can't change that. I excuse my thoughts and behaviour by telling myself we're not human, and we don't need to live by anyone's standards but our own. The issue is, there're very human reactions happening between us whatever and whoever we are. The emotional and physical tie joins us as strongly as whatever else links us.

Now this has happened with Ewan, I need to talk to the guys about this. We need to be clear what's happening and how we deal with the situation.

I head downstairs where the guys sit around in the large lounge room. I squish myself between Joss and Ewan on the sofa, and they both shuffle closer. Heath's in an armchair opposite, feet on the table, focused on his phone, and Xander sits upright in the opposite chair. The TV is off, and the nearby low coffee table clear. I'm still amused by Joss's constant tidying. The early sun shines through the large window, the light picking up dust in the air.

"We need a debrief on what happened last night," Xander says and taps his phone on his leg. "Don't we, Ewan?"

Ewan and I both snap our heads to look at Xander. A muscle in his cheek twitches as he continues, fighting amusement at our reaction, "I mean Vee proving she's the most powerful person sitting in this room. Isn't she? Heath filled me in on what Vee told him happened last night. At the demons' house, I mean."

"Oh. Right." Ewan relaxes again. "Yeah."

Joss wraps an arm around my shoulders. "I think it's awesome. If we harness this, we'll be unstoppable."

"I wouldn't get too cocky," puts in Heath. "Early days. How do you feel about what happened, Vee? Do you think you can control it?"

"None of us could early on," puts in Xander. "It's a learning process." He turns to me. "Let me get this straight, Vee. You used mine, Joss, and Heath's powers. But not Ewan's?"

"Not this time. I felt you all but I think maybe Ewan's harder." I smack Joss on the knee as he sniggers like a twelve-year-old. "Harder for me to tune into, dumbass. I don't know. Perhaps I react with the powers I need to use."

"Hmm." Xander continues to tap his phone. "You had difficulty with Ewan, huh?" I glare at his continued amusement and he shakes his head at me. "Yeah, maybe next time Ewan's power will come through."

"Maybe she has his computer skills?" suggests Joss.

"Ewan and her can sit down later and take a look at what they have," Heath says.

"More one-on-one time for them both?" Xander cocks a brow.

"I love that Vee has some War power," retorts Ewan. "She can balance out your attitude."

"Vee has something to match all of us," says Heath. "Maybe if she works with each of us, we can figure out how far her powers go."

I break my silence. "I'm happy this is my power. I'm glad I'm at the centre of you all; I feel it explains what's happening between us, and I don't feel crap about it anymore. Xander began to make me feel like I'd cause too much trouble between the four of you. Instead I think this unites you."

"One big happy family." Joss grins, and Heath frowns at him. "No, I mean it. We live as a family, and now we've a new member."

Here goes nothing... I clear my throat, like a politician about to make an important speech. "I need to know what's okay in this situation. We're all aware of our bond, and I have to be sure where I fit into that. You guys all love each other like brothers." I pause. "But I don't feel like a sister to you. I'm pulled to every one of you, and this is causing issues, isn't it?"

Joss shrugs against my shoulders. "No issue to me. You can have sex with whoever you like."

"I'm not just talking about sex!" I protest. "Physically and emotionally."

Heath places his phone down. "What are you talking about here, Vee?"

"I don't want to depend on you—any of you, and as soon as I let one of you closer than the others, I know the protectiveness and maybe possessiveness will join that. I haven't had many successful relationships, not just because of the truth/lie thing, but because I don't want to be defined as part of a couple. Here, I feel I'm part of you all. I care about you all, whether that's this supernatural bond, or more, I'm not sure yet."

"All? Even Mr Rude Bastard?" asks Joss.

I turn my head to Xander, enjoying his stunned look. "Sweetheart, I don't buy into that. They might all want a piece of the action, but I'm not getting involved."

"All good," I say. Will this man ever understand I know he's lying? "But please, can I lay this on the table? I have to live with you all, there're strong feelings and mutual attraction. But I won't choose one of you. I can't be that. We can't do that."

"So what are you suggesting?" Joss asks, eyes shining with fun. "Are you going to put us on rotation? Two days of the week each? Maybe it's good Xander isn't interested because you'll have a day to rest."

He's only half joking, and I flick him on the nose. "Not. Just. About. Sex. But we're living in close proximity. Things will happen if we let them, won't they? I'm just saying, if they do, it doesn't mean I've chosen."

Jesus, I sound bad. Wrong even. I run both hands through my hair. "I'm as confused as you are. This behaviour isn't like me, but then I'm not the old Vee, am I?"

Joss stretches out his long legs and places his feet on the table. "I already said I'm okay with whatever."

"Heath?" I ask.

He scratches an eye. "Logical. Not a hundred percent sure how I feel, but I accept what you're saying."

Ewan tips his head. "After last night, I'm not gonna say no. I'm here when you need me, whatever you need me for."

Heath's head jerks up. "Last night?"

Ewan looks over at me, and Joss pipes up. "Let me put it this way. She didn't sleep in my bedroom, Heath.."

"Oh." He blows air into his cheeks and looks down at his phone. I dip my head to see what he's thinking, but his features are unreadable.

"Ewan and me spent some time together," I say to Joss. "Interpret that how you want."

"I was going to say you have to be truthful with us

about everything if this is to work, but I guess there's no need," says Joss with a laugh.

"I love different things about each of you," I reply.

Xander makes a soft sound in his throat. "Love. Bullshit. Co-dependency multiplied by four. Great."

"You're very suspicious of me, aren't you, Xander?" I ask.

"No. I just want to figure this situation the hell out. Can we talk about more than your romantic aspirations, Vee?"

I scowl. "I think this is important, and like I said, I'm talking about more than sex. I mean companionship too, how the synergy between us means we'll always live together as five and never 'two plus three.'"

Xander jabs a finger at each of us. "You know what's important? Tracking down the person behind the plot to kill Portia. Finding out how far our Mr Big's influence spreads because there's a lot of shit going down without your fours' obsession with screwing each other." He shakes his head. "Heath. Joss. Maybe you should get it out of your system. Ewan obviously has. Both of you with her, or separately, I don't care."

Ewan stares ahead and I wish I knew what words he's holding back right now. I stand. "If you want to drag this down to that level, fine. But I don't think it's as simple as you say."

"Yeah? I told you the other night what the deal would be between me and you. That hasn't changed."

"I heard. Loud and clear."

"The lady doth protest too much, methinks," says Joss and raises both brows at Xander.

Joss quoting Shakespeare—and correctly? I'll add that to the list of this week's shocking occurrences.

Heath huffs. "I think this is exactly why Vee's having the conversation, Xander. Now we know the score, we move on. She's here for important reasons, and we need to remain unified."

"How about we show her the picture?" announces Joss and receives a sharp *no* from Xander and Ewan. Heath shakes his head at him.

"What picture?" I ask.

"Nothing. Just something Joss found in a book when he was researching. It's not important," says Xander, eyes on Joss.

"But aren't we telling her everything? Now I know how powerful she is, I'm not upsetting Vee," he replies.

"It's a bloody picture, Joss," retorts Heath. "It really doesn't mean anything."

"Well, obviously it does if you're all making such a big deal out of it." I rub my forehead. "Is it of me?"

"Fine, just get the book," says Xander.

Joss slaps his hands on his legs and stands, before heading out the door towards the back of the house. I've peeked into the room back there before—a study with walls lined by shelves and books I'm curious to read. I rest my head on Ewan's shoulder and look over to the ever-friendly Xander.

"What next?" I ask him.

"We're at a dead end. Time to start questioning some of the other supes," he replies.

"Supes? Oh. Like the vampires or shifters or whoever?" I shiver slightly.

"Maybe. Plus, Portia wants us over tonight for one of her so-called dinner parties," replies Xander.

Did I hear correctly? "Dinner party?"

"Yeah, don't be fooled. She usually has an agenda when she invites us," says Ewan.

"Besides trying to get into Xander's pants," puts in Heath.

Oh god, too funny. I'd love to see *that*.

"Guys!" Joss's urgent voice comes from the direction he walked. "I think you need to see this."

All three jump to their feet, a well-rehearsed call to action as Xander storms ahead through the lounge room door. Heath puts out a hand to try to stop me following, but drops it when I meet his action with a filthy look.

I edge along behind them, and as we reach the front hallway I look between Heath and Ewan. "Front door was open," says Joss, who's standing in the entrance.

"And?" asks Xander.

Joss screws up his face and nods to something I can't see, outside. Xander pulls himself straight and strides over. I wait for his brusque instructions to us, but as soon as he steps onto the path, he halts.

Xander speechless?

Heart speeding, I follow Heath and Ewan, who barricade themselves together in the doorway so I can't pass. I duck beneath their arms and immediately wish I hadn't.

On the gravelled drive way, a body lies on the floor a few feet away, beside Heath's car. I'm close enough to see a body that's disfigured and bloody to the point I can't tell if it's male or female, or human. I clasp a hand over my mouth, fighting back a reaction that would get me noticed and pushed away from the situation. There's no bird song to interrupt the silence gripping us all. I glance at the guys; their faces are expressionless. How can they not be moved by this? Or is this as close as they get to shock?

I don't want to look again, but the guys' continued staring draws my eyes back in the body's direction. My scalp prickles and cold trickles down my spine spreading into my veins. Someone has smeared blood across the bonnet and written two words on the white paintwork:

GUESS WHO?

The Four Horsemen series continues with *Hunted*.

The Secret of the Missing Cat

I've received emails and messages from concerned (and some upset) readers who missed what happened to Vee's cat in *Legacy*. In *Legacy*, she does say to herself that the cat had left her for the neighbours. He wasn't left in a burning flat!

But, as someone who owns three cats, I could understand their concerns and decided to write a short scene that takes place close to the beginning of *Bound*.

Thiswill hopefully bring some closure for Vee, the cat and the readers...

VEE

Did I expect the place to disappear along with my old life?

I stare at the furniture shop, with my flat in the same position above it, and my car parked in the lane around the back. I stand outside Heath's car and clutch the tissue inside my jacket pockets. I attempt to hide how freaked out I am as I'm confronted by the reality the guys told me didn't exist.

There's no fooling Joss. He places a hand on my arm, concerned eyes studying my face. "You okay?"

"I think so. It's as if I'm looking at a stranger's flat. I thought I'd feel like I was coming home but... no."

"Do you want to go inside?"

I shake my head as my pulse quickens. "No. Not today. We can sort everything out another time."

Heath leans over the low brick wall between the street and the yard behind the shop. His combat jacket and T-shirt ride up revealing a toned back and the oh-so-gropeable ass in his dark denim jeans. "Where did you last see your cat?" he calls.

"Chasing another cat up the street," I reply.

Heath steps back again. "He's obviously not hanging around your flat pining for you."

I scowl. "I'm aware of that. I told you, my cat stopped coming home altogether a week before I met you guys. For the month leading up to that, he rarely appeared."

"Are you sure he was your cat?" Joss asks.

"What? Of course, he was! I don't randomly abduct animals and force them to live with me."

Heath and Joss glance at each other; a bloody annoying habit they all have when I know I'm excluded from something. I poke Joss in the stomach – or attempt to since solid muscle greets me. "Stop that! What's wrong?"

"How old's your cat, Vee?" he asks in a quiet voice.

"I adopted him from the shelter a year ago," I retort. "He isn't a false memory. He's my cat."

"Or was," mutters Heath. "What are you going to do if we find him?"

I open my mouth to answer, but I don't have one. Take the cat back to the guys' property? And then what happens when I need to go away, since they've made it clear we're not staying in the area permanently? Plus, aren't cats freaked out by moving home? What if he tries to return to his new family and doesn't make it?

"Call for the cat, Heath," says Joss. "He might be scared and hiding."

"More like enjoying life in someone's house," he mutters. "Vee, you call him."

What's with Heath's reluctance and Joss's unsuppressed amusement? Oh, right. *His name.* "Fine. I will."

Scalp prickling under their scrutiny, I wander behind the row of shops to the narrow laneway. "Bacon!"

Joss erupts into laughter, and I shoot him a filthy look. He holds his hands up. "Sorry, but seriously? Bacon? No wonder he fled. Probably thought you were going to make breakfast out of him."

"It was his name at the shelter. I didn't want to change it," I retort.

Heath approaches and wraps an arm around my shoulders. He hugs me to his warm chest, the scent I associate with head-spinning kisses moving over me. "I know you're worried. Ignore dumbass taking the piss."

"I am not! It's just funny, okay?" Joss approaches too and touches my face. "I promise not to laugh at your cat's hilarious name again."

I pout. "*You* call for him, then."

"Huh?"

Now it's Heath's turn to snigger.

"The cat? Go on," I challenge.

Joss purses his lips and glances around furtively. The surroundings are empty of everything but parked cars, rubbish gathering in the drains, and us.

"Bacon," he says in barely a whisper.

Heath's laughter matches Joss's from earlier, and I duck from under his arm. "This is getting us nowhere! I'm going to check out the neighbour's place."

Leaving the comedians behind, I stride in the direction of the terraced row of houses until I reach the narrow, gated backyards consisting of concrete pavers or uneven ground. I halt in front of a yard with washing pegged to the line and look over the wall at the net curtains in the kitchen window. I've seen Bacon hanging out in this yard, so I count how many houses to the end, and march around to the path leading along the front of the houses.

My Horsemen protectors follow. A young woman passing, with a child in a stroller, double takes. They're oblivious, focused on me. I smile a little too smugly when she stares at me in disbelief. *Yep, they're mine. Both of them.*

"This is the one," I say.

The front windows contain the same yellowing net curtains as the rear, and a sunflower grows in a terracotta pot by the blue door. What was once a lawn is now muddy with sparse grass, and a tarmac path leads to the door. There's a faded plastic sand box on one side, and two small bikes resting against the red brick on the other.

I search for a doorbell. None. Taking a nervous breath, I rap on the door.

I'm about to knock for the second time when a woman answers. She has curly blonde hair and dark circles beneath her eyes, dressed in baggy pants and a cardigan over a T-shirt. She holds a toddler against her hip; a young girl with brown hair who grips her mother's shirt in one hand and a doll in another.

The woman eyes us suspiciously. "Yes?"

"Um. Sorry to bother you, but –" I begin.

"What are you selling? I don't want to buy anything." She hitches the girl further up her hip and makes to close the door, her wary look switching to Joss and Heath, who flank me.

"No. I'm looking for my cat."

The woman pauses. "Cat? What does it look like?"

Hope rises. I bet the ungrateful animal *did* move here. "Black. But he has one white paw." I indicate my right hand. "He should have a red collar too."

"The black cat's yours?" she asks. "I thought he was a stray."

"He's a bit fat to be a stray," I retort. His weight gain over the last few month confirmed to me he has another – if not several more – homes to dine at.

"He's always hungry when he comes here," she replies.

Is she suggesting I neglect my cat? "He's always hungry, full stop."

The woman bites the corner of her lip, distracted by the godlike men either side of me. "You have quite a search party for one cat."

"Just ask her outright," says Heath gracing her with a friendly smile. "I'm sure if this lovely lady knows where your cat is she'll tell you."

The woman's cheeks redden at his attention, but I understand Heath's hint.

"Have you seen my cat?" I ask her outright.

"Yes. The cat's inside." The woman blinks. "With my daughter. Wait there."

She disappears inside the house, closing the door

with a click. I shuffle from foot to foot as I wait, hoping the cat is Bacon.

"What are you going to do if it is him?" asks Joss again. "Xander would lose his shit if we took a cat home."

Which tempts me to do exactly that. But taking Bacon to my new home would be unfair. I'll need to join the Horsemen on their "trips away", and who'll look after a cat then?

We glance at each other as voices rise in the house and a child wails. The woman returns, followed by a blonde-haired girl around three years old. She cradles a black cat in her arms as if he were a baby, and Bacon's unmistakable white paw touches her face. Guilt twinges when I spot the tears streaking the girls cheeks.

"Is this him?" asks the woman.

Bacon looks at me, not struggling against the girl's hold, and with no sign of interest. *Bloody cats.*

"Have you come for Blackie?" she asks and sniffs. "He's my cat." I wince for Bacon as the girl squeezes him tighter.

"Give Blackie to the lady," says the woman and places a hand on the girl's head. "He belongs to her, and she loves him too. The lady wants to take her cat home."

"But he came to live with me," the girl protests. "He doesn't want to go home!"

Ah, crap. The guys either side of me remain mute. Why did they come with me if they weren't going to help?

"Maybe put him down?" I suggest. "He doesn't look comfortable."

The teary girl half-drops Bacon to the floor who rubs himself around her legs. Again, no response to me. I slide a hand down my face. This situation is awkward and not what I expected. What do I do?

"The cat's always here," says the woman. "He follows Maisie everywhere and sleeps on her bed. If you take him, he'll probably come back."

She's right, another reason I can't take him to the guys' place. I've heard about cats walking miles to return to their homes and territory. "Hang on."

I turn to a perturbed looking Heath. "What do I do?" I whisper.

"I don't know anything about cats. Joss?"

"She really loves him," he says in a low voice. "If uh... Bacon likes living here you know he'll be safe."

"But I want him too." My words are almost a whine as if I'm a girl cut up over a broken relationship. Bacon left me for somewhere and someone he prefers.

Joss takes my hand and squeezes. "Maybe he hated his name, and that's why he ran away."

I scowl and slap his hand away. "Ha ha."

"What's his real name?" asks the woman.

My heart hurts as I look down at the wide-eyed girl, the one whose new pet I could take away from her.

No. he should stay here. This way, I can be sure he's safe. With me, he won't be.

"Blackie," I say.

The girl's smile brings sunshine into the shadows of my day.

I fight the lump in my throat as we walk away with reassurances from the woman, who finally introduced

BONUS SCENE

herself as Meg, that the newly named Blackie would be safe with them.

On the drive home, I rest my head on Joss's shoulder, his hand on my knee, and close my eyes. Both guys fussed over me when we walked away from the house. Their hugs were welcome, but I need to put him out of my mind. I repeat to myself he's better and happier with Maisie.

Heath and Joss don't mention my cat again.

Halfway home, the car veers off the road, and I open my eyes. A petrol station forecourt comes into view, and Heath stops his car at a pump.

"How often do you think the original Horsemen had to refuel?" I ask with a smile.

"Original Horsemen?"

"The Four Horsemen. Men on horses, not in SUVs. Do you think their horses were magical?"

Heath shakes his head at me. "That's a story, remember."

"I know, I was kidding."

I glance at Joss who shrugs at Heath's unimpressed response. "Did you know Heath can't ride a horse? We tried once."

"I'm trying hard not to laugh here," I say. "The Horseman who can't ride a horse."

"Watching what happened when you tried was funnier, huh, Heath?"

Heath opens the car door. "You're not as hilarious as you think, Joss. I'll fill the car, and we can head home."

"I want to tell Xander we have the cat just to see his reaction," says Joss. "Man, that would be hilarious."

Heath shakes his head but fights a smile too. *Tempting idea.*

The car door clunks closed, and I watch as Heath stands by the car and fills the tank, eyes to the sky. I look out too, at the cars lined up around, and at the people walking in and out of the small store attached, or leaving with snacks. Business people in company cars, mothers in SUVs, tradesmen in white vans. Ordinary people; normal lives.

People with no idea what lives amongst them.

I shuffle down and cover my face; I don't want to take in any more of the real world today.

"I understand," whispers Joss and pulls fingers from my face. "You don't need to pretend you're okay."

His green eyes, soft with concern, look into mine as he tips my chin with his thumb and forefinger. He places a kiss on my forehead, at a spot between my eyes, before hugging me to him.

After a few silent moments he says, "If we ever capture a hellhound to keep as a pet, you're not naming it, okay?"

"Hellhound? Do they exist?" I ask, face against his chest.

Joss chuckles. "No. Well, I don't think so. I haven't met one yet."

I groan. "Heath's right, you're not as funny as you think."

Joss strokes my cheek with his thumb, and I close my eyes again. Leaving behind Bacon in the girl's safe, sticky, hands brings a finality to my switch from Vee to the Fifth.

My cat was the last part of my old life, and now he's gone.

ACKNOWLEDGMENTS

A special thanks to Angel Lawson for the help and support, and for sharing so much.

I've been welcomed into the reverse harem community by such a wonderful group of people and want to thank them too. Thanks especially to Ashley Leanne Pelham and Soobee Dewson for their support with launching Legacy.

Thanks especially to all the lovely readers who joined the Four Horsemen readers group and talk to me on a daily basis so I have some social communication!

Thank you to Krys Janae from TakeCover Designs for designing such a beautiful series of covers.

And again, thanks to Peggy for her editing excellence and friendship.

One last thanks to everybody who read Legacy and enjoyed the story enough to recommend to others and buy the next book.

ABOUT THE AUTHOR

LJ Swallow is a USA Today bestselling paranormal romance and urban fantasy author who is the alter-ego of bestselling contemporary romance author Lisa Swallow.

Giving in to her dark side, LJ spends time creating worlds filled with supernatural creatures who don't fit the norm, and heroines who are more likely to kick ass than sit on theirs.

Newsletter
http://madmimi.com/signups/367776/join

For more information:
ljswallow.com
lisa@lisaswallow.net

Printed in Great Britain
by Amazon